FAST AND CURIOUS

A NEW WINDMILL BOOK OF SHORT STORIES

EDITED BY MIKE ROYSTON

Heinemann
New Windmills

Heinemann Educational Publishers
Halley Court, Jordan Hill, Oxford OX2 8EJ
A division of Reed Educational and Professional Publishing Ltd

OXFORD MELBOURNE AUCKLAND
JOHANNESBURG BLANTYRE GABORONE
IBADAN PORTSMOUTH (NH) USA CHICAGO

03
10 9 8 7 6 5

ISBN 0 435 13045 5

Acknowledgements
The Editor and Publishers would like to thank the following for permission to use
copyright material:

The Agency (London) Ltd for 'Brian and the Brain' from *Sensational Cyber Stories*, published
by Transworld Publishers Ltd 1997. Copyright © Janet Burchett and Sara Vogler 1997. All rights
reserved and enquiries to The Agency (London) Ltd, 24 Pottery Lane, London W11 4LZ, p1;
Dennis Hamley for 'Faces' from *Shirt off a Hanged Man's Back* published by Andre Deutsch
1984, first published in this version 1999. Copyright © Dennis Hamley 1999, p15; Neil Arksey
for 'Banana' from *Football Fever* ed. Tony Bradman, published by Transworld Publishers Ltd.
Copyright © Neil Arksey 1998, p19; 'The Bakerloo Flea', reprinted by permission of The Peters,
Fraser and Dunlop Group Limited on behalf of Michael Rosen, © Michael Rosen, p31; Orion
Children's Books for 'Star Pupil' by Lorna Read from *Out of this World* ed. Wendy Cooling in the
Quids for Kids series, published by Orion Children's books 1997, p40; Orion Children's Books
for 'Needle' by Alan Gibbons from *On the Run* ed. Wendy Cooling in the *Quids for Kids* series,
published by Orion Children's Books 1997, p52; Redvers Brandling for 'Mayday' © Redvers
Brandling 1994, p60; Orion Children's Books for 'Worms' by John Gatehouse from *Bad Dreams*
ed. Wendy Cooling in the *Quids for Kids* series, published by Orion Children's Books 1997, p67;
Egmont Children's Books for 'Cocky and Clive' by Robert Swindells © Robert Swindells, from
Best of Friends ed. Valerie Bierman, published by Methuen Children's Books 1995, p78; Orion
Children's Books for 'Chicken' by Mary Hoffman from *Dare You* ed. Wendy Cooling in the
Quids for Kids series, published by Orion Children's Books 1997, p87; Rogers, Coleridge and
White Ltd for 'Virtually True' by Paul Stewart from *Sensational Cyber Stories* published by
Transworld Publishers Ltd 1997. Copyright © Paul Stewart 1997, p103.

The Publishers have made every effort to trace the copyright holders, but if they have
inadvertently overlooked any, they will be pleased to make the necessary arrangements at
the first opportunity.

Cover design by The Point
Cover illustration by John Leigh
Illustrations by Bob Wilson, Neil Parker, Philip Bannister and Mark Oliver
Typeset by 🐦 Tek-Art, Croydon, Surrey
Printed and bound in the United Kingdom by Clays Ltd, St Ives plc

Contents

Introduction   v

Brian and the Brain – Janet Burchett and Sara Vogler   1

Faces – Dennis Hamley   15

Banana – Neil Arksey   19

The Bakerloo Flea – Michael Rosen   31

Star Pupil – Lorna Read   40

Needle – Alan Gibbons   52

Mayday! – Redvers Brandling   60

Worms – John Gatehouse   67

Cocky and Clive – Robert Swindells   78

Chicken – Mary Hoffman   87

Barney – Will Stanton   98

Virtually True – Paul Stewart   103

Activities   117

Introduction

What is *your* recipe for an appetizing story? Most people's ingredients include: plenty of action, interesting characters, enough suspense to keep you reading, and a strong ending which ties everything together.

The twelve stories in *Fast and Curious* have been mixed from these ingredients. They are all on different subjects. They offer you a varied reading menu from which to choose stories suited to your own particular taste. The idea is that, like a good meal, they should leave you feeling satisfied – but looking forward to the next one.

In this collection the writers start by asking the same basic question – 'What happens when . . . ?' For instance: what happens when a teenager struggling with school work finds that the family computer is able to re-program his mind? *Brian and the Brain* shows you. What happens when a newcomer in the class announces he's an alien from planet Karn? Find out in *Star Pupil*.

Other stories introduce you to characters and situations you might recognize from everyday life – like *Needle*, which shows how a victim fights back against school bullies by trying to beat them at their own game. Or *Chicken*, where an escalating series of dares leads the boys in a gang into terrible danger. Or *Banana*, the story of the brilliant goalkeeper who is kept out of the team because he's too small, until . . .

You will find large slices of humour in this collection. None of the stories are heavy either in their style or content. Some, like *Barney* and *Cocky and Clive*, are about serious subjects but their writers don't preach at you. They let you make up your own mind about things you may not have thought of in quite the same way before.

This book aims to provide you with entertaining stories which are equally good to listen to, to read aloud, or to read silently. They're not meant for tests or exams but to be enjoyable in their own right. If you find that they *are*, don't keep it to yourself. Tell others!

Mike Royston

Brian and the Brain
Janet Burchett and Sara Vogler

Brian had homework. It was writing, and writing was a bit of a problem for Brian. Whatever he produced, it would look as if a drunken spider had staggered across the page. Whatever he produced, he knew what Miss Spenshaw would say.

'It may be the best work in the history of the school, Brian, but as I can't read it we shall never know, shall we? Perhaps we could fax it off to Beijing for a translation.'

There's nothing like a good joke, thought Brian, and that's nothing like a good joke.

Of course, there would be no problem if he could do it on the computer. But last week, while he'd been trying to install *Attack of the Killer Klingfilms*, Mum's story *Ellie and the Elves Go Skipping* had somehow got deleted. She'd been about to send it off to her publisher. Brian felt it was unfair. Mum had claimed that it was his fault. But the whole family knew what the computer was like. An eccentric, cranky old thing. Second-hand from the eccentric cranky old woman down the road, 'The Brain' had come into the family like an intelligent but unreliable dog. You never knew if it was going to lick, bite or wee on the carpet. You touched it at your peril. Dad wouldn't go near it. Not since the mouse had given him an electric shock.

The Brain had no sense of humour. In the face of the most ridiculous spelling mistake it would merely add a solemn red line underneath. It ignored Brian's expertise at space games – even when he got top of the top ten. And sometimes it would announce unexpectedly that you had performed an illegal operation and the program would now be closed down, or else. Brian often wondered what it would do – send the computer police round? He thought about what they would look like. Would they knock politely or beat your door down?

But when The Brain swallowed Ellie, along with twenty-four of her elfin friends, Brian's mother had gently discouraged him from using it for a while.

'If you ever touch that machine again, I will personally come into your assembly and read *Ellie and the Elves Go to the Farm* – with sound effects.'

So Brian thought he would give technology a miss for a few days.

But this was serious. The homework had to be in tomorrow. Otherwise, Miss Spenshaw had said, he could do it during football practice. Luckily, Mum was out in the garden having a fight with the ivy. She'd be ages. The ivy always won in the end. There was plenty of time to finish a game of *Space Bowls* and thrash out the homework too.

But first he had to put the wet sponges in Grace's bed and stick the plastic spider on her mirror. It was nearly a week since he'd glued her shoes to the bedroom floor. He mustn't let standards slip. When he got back to the computer he felt that a quick game of *Space Bowls* would loosen up his fingers nicely. He made level thirty-seven before being blown to pieces. Not bad. Now for the essay. Or should he have a quick game of *Giant Aphids of Andromeda*? No, he must be strong. He resigned himself to the unpleasant task ahead.

'All About Me'. How stupid. It was like being five again. Why couldn't Miss Spenshaw let him write about 'How to be World Champion at *Marauding Martians*'? Or, 'My Hundred Best Practical Jokes'? He sighed, slumped down in his seat and typed:

<u>all abot me bye Brain Bossley</u>
PlEase see work done 6 weeks ago when
yoooooooou were off with the chicken pox
and WE HaD thAt naFF SUPPLy teacher who
kept falling aSleep. zzzzzzzzzzzzzz. i
haven't cHanGEd snincE then. i thank you.

He looked up and read what he'd written. Keyboard skills were not his strong point but at least she'd be able to read it. The Brain had put red lines under nearly every word. Brian ignored them. He didn't need keyboard skills, not when he was so ace with the mouse and the joystick. Then he remembered. He had to finish with 'My Greatest Wish'. He'd make them all laugh. He thought he might wish to be Mike Megabyte, hero of *Alien Bashers Anon*. He stared at the screen. He noticed he'd spelt his name wrong – Brain. That was it! Never mind Mike Megabyte, he'd have the lot. He'd have the entire brain of the computer. He'd reach level 1027 of *Thundering Terrapins* before they knew what had hit them. He wouldn't have to struggle with his handwriting. He might even find maths easier if he could understand it. And he'd probably make even quicker quips. Yes, he'd have them rolling in the aisles. He'd probably get into *The Guinness Book of Records* – the Boy with a Brain the Size of Jupiter. But that sort of thing only happened in *Nova-nerds from Neptune* where you picked up extra brain-power as you went along. Slipping further down in his seat, he carried on typing.

i wish to swOp brains with my cOmpouter.

He grabbed the mouse to click on 'print'. But the moment he did so he felt a weird sensation in his head. It was as if someone had flushed his brain. He could feel it emptying like a toilet cistern. Then, an army of electronic ants seemed to march from the mouse, into his fingers, up his arm and finally into his skull.

The back door banged.

'What are you up to, Brian?' shouted Mum. 'I hope you're not on that computer.'

Brian mechanically tidied up the computer table, tucked in the chair and marched up to bed without a word.

Next morning, Mum came in to give Brian the first of his time checks and increasingly unpleasant threats. She pulled back the curtains.

'Welcome to Windows,' said a loud voice behind her. She swung round. Brian was standing, fully dressed, beside an immaculately made bed. Mum couldn't believe it. She staggered out. Brian, feeling rather odd, marched down to breakfast behind her.

He stared at his cereal.

'There are two hundred and fifty-six Corn Crunchies in my bowl. The square root of two hundred and fifty-six is sixteen. Therefore it will only take me sixteen spoonfuls of sixteen Corn Crunchies to finish my cereal – with no remainder.'

'That was impressive, Brian,' said Dad when he'd checked the arithmetic on the back of an envelope. He looked at his son. 'Are you OK, Brian? You're looking a bit pale.'

Brian considered this. He certainly did feel different this morning. And more surprisingly still, he found he wasn't interested in retrieving the spider and sponges before Grace threw them away. That all seemed rather childish and totally irrelevant now. But then, of course, when you had 1.6 gigabytes and 100 megahertz, who needed jokes and space games? Maths, data, memory – that was the real world.

'Brian can't even add up,' said his sister grumpily. She'd had a bad night. 'He's got a brain the size of a Ricicle. He must've got it off the back of the cereal packet. I'm fed up with Corn Crunchies, Mum. Haven't we got anything else?'

'Did you know,' Brian piped up to his own surprise, 'just one click brings down a menu?'

His family ignored him. They were used to his jokes.

'One of these days,' Mum was saying to anyone who would listen, 'I'm going wallpaper shopping. I'm fed up with these spots. If I don't watch out, I'm going to find myself counting them . . .'

'There are two million, one hundred and sixty thousand, three hundred and thirty-seven spots on the kitchen walls,' announced Brian. Mum put her hand on his forehead.

'Are you feeling all right, Brian?' she asked.

'Everything is in normal view, thank you,' said Brian. 'And please call me Brain.'

He marched off to school.

Brian sat at his table. He laid out his pens, rulers and rubbers in neat rows. He finally managed to find his books in the clutter of his drawer, and arranged them symmetrically in front of him. Now he had customized his desktop, he looked up – ready and waiting to impress.

'Brian Bossley,' said Miss Spenshaw sternly, 'if it's not too much to ask, could I have your homework please?'

'The file cannot be found,' said Brian, staring squarely at her. 'Please check that the correct file name has been entered.'

The class began to titter. Brian, the school clown, never failed. And more impressive, Brian was keeping a straight face.

'That's enough, Brian,' said Miss Spenshaw. 'I want to see "All About Me" – NOW!'

'Correct file name has been entered,' replied Brian. 'Ready to print. And please call me Brain.'

The class giggled. But for some reason Brian didn't look round with his usual merry grin. Miss Spenshaw stared. She hadn't expected him to do as he was told. Brian hadn't expected to do as he was told either. But he had to – she had issued a command.

He took a clean sheet of paper and carefully sharpened a pencil. He did a mental spell check, sorted out the capital letters and completed a word count. He wondered why he had written this rubbish. It was pathetic for a boy with a brain the size of Jupiter.

'File name "All About Me" . . . font – extremely untidy . . . double space . . . font size – overlarge, twenty-six.'

With the speed of a printer, his work appeared on the paper. Only the ending had changed:

```
Computers have no need for wishes, only
commands. Tip of the day — did you know
you can speed up your working efficiency
with extra megabytes?
```

With that, Brian suddenly got up and walked round the classroom collecting all the books. He put them into brown folders.

'What are you doing?' asked Miss Spenshaw.

'All the work has now been saved in files,' announced Brian. The class started laughing.

'Good old Brian,' said Luke. 'He never fails.'

Brian felt a surge of irritation.

'Please call me Brain,' he snapped.

Meanwhile at home, Mum switched on the computer to do some work. The machine made a dreadful grinding noise.

'Wotcha!' read the screen.

Mum was surprised. Brian must have learnt how to customize the screen saver at last.

'Beep!'

The whole class jumped. Brian didn't usually go in for beeping.

'To gracebossley from williamwigeon@StevenageBird Sanctuary.Co.UK. Spoonbills safely hatched. Mother and chicks doing well,' Brian announced.

Everyone fell about. Gradually the laughter died down as the kids realized that Brian wasn't joking. Brian ignored them and carried on with his maths.

'Brian . . . Brian!'

'Ready, Miss Spenshaw.'

'Thank you for sharing that with us, Brian. Perhaps you will kindly explain yourself.'

'Just delivering an e-mail message. And please call me Brain.'

Miss Spenshaw walked over and peered at Brian's work. Her jaw dropped down to her knees. Although it was as untidy as ever, it was all correct and he was on page twenty-two already.

Mum wasn't getting much work done. Ellie and the Elves hadn't finished packing their picnic basket yet. She had hoped to get them to the woods before lunch. She kept being interrupted by prompt boxes:

```
? What's for tea ?
```

and

```
! This story is soooooo bor-ing !
```

and

```
?  Have  you  heard  the  one  about  the
rabbit  and  the  spirit  level  ?
```

The computer had even called her Mum twice and claimed it was too tired to do any work. Mum wished she had gone wallpaper shopping instead.

At break-time, Luke skidded up to Brian, hands out ready for the usual joystick wrist-actions and synchronized air-mousing. But Brian ignored him. He'd only been out there for three minutes and forty-eight point nine seconds and he'd already been pestered six times by children asking him to tell them jokes. No one wanted Encarta. No one needed a bar chart. No one even asked after his database. He wanted to fulfil commands, save, edit, insert and take messages. He wanted to show them what he could do.

'Beep! To mrjohnbossley from robbie.reliant@dodgy motors.Co.UK. Ford Capri E reg. Excellent condition. Egg yellow with green doors . . .'

'You're no fun any more, Brian Bossley,' said Luke. 'Your jokes are awful – and you've turned into a boffin.'

Brian considered the matter.

'Boffin. Not found in thesaurus. Suggest change to bodkin or bog.'

'You swot!' shouted Luke.

'Swot,' said Brian. 'No synonyms found. And please call me Brain.'

Luke stormed off. Brian stood there, blinking. Then, from somewhere deep down came an illogical thought. Brian ignored it at first. He thought it was the screen saver scrolling across his vision.

```
Call  Luke  back  and  tell  him  it's  all  a
joke.  Call  Luke  back  and  tell  him  .  .  .
```

Brian tried to delete it but it wouldn't go. It kept on scrolling. It bothered him. It rattled his RAM.

Mum had gone past the point of calling the computer words you wouldn't find in any spell check. Now she sat there in silence. She was even thinking about writing her story by hand. The computer had given up its irritating messages, but now her entire story had gone missing. She searched frantically and finally found it. She opened the file. Up came the title – *Ellie and the Elves Get Beaten Up*. There followed grisly descriptions of packs of avenging pixies and disembowelled elves hanging from trees. Then a prompt box appeared.

! Well that's disposed of Ellie and the Elves. Let's play Vlad the Inhaler. It's a bit of a wheeze. You'll like it if you try it, Mum !

'Just wait till I get my hands on that boy,' muttered Brian's mother.

By quarter past eleven, Brian had finished his year's work.
'Beep!'
'Brian, stop that!'
'To mrsevangelinebossley from R.T.Choke@Veg-U-Like.recipes.Co.UK. Spinach and Aubergine Burger. First chop the spinach. Then soak the aubergines in orange juice . . .'
'I suppose he thinks that's funny,' Luke called out. 'But it's not. He's lost his sense of humour.'
Brian tried to access C:\Sense.of.humour. No file found. It bothered him. He kept searching. Another message unexpectedly scrolled across.

Why aren't they laughing any more? Why
aren't they laughing . . .

Brian, the boy with a brain the size of Jupiter, couldn't
understand why this was so important to him. But
somehow it was. If he couldn't sort it out he might have
to shut down – and then what?

'Beep!'

He didn't want to give the next message but he
couldn't stop himself.

'To miss.cuddlekins.spenshaw from your tiger.-cyril.
blake@County.High.School.UK . . .'

'Brian! I'm warning you!'

'Looking forward to our date tonight and lots of
snoodling . . .'

'Brian. Go to the office at once and tell them to take
your temperature.'

Brian marched to the office. When he got there, Mrs
Thompson, the school secretary, was updating the
database. He stepped purposefully forward to assist.
Instead a thermometer was inserted in his mouth.

'Keep still and don't bite it,' said Mrs Thompson.

Brian sat on the sick chair. He wanted to sort out this
strange feeling. It did not compute properly. He didn't
like his megabytes being muddled. Having the brain of a
computer wasn't half as good as he'd thought. There was
something seriously wrong. A brain the size of Jupiter
was all very well but there was something missing.

I feel lonely. Where are my friends? I
feel lonely. Where are my friends?

came the message from somewhere. Brian checked his
hard drive for an error. The message changed.

```
I can't stand this any more. I can't
stand this any more. I can't stand
this . . .
```

Now he knew what the problem was. Brian was rejecting The Brain. He needed to be Brian, King Joker and Champion Space Bowler. He tried to make contact with the home terminal. He announced the message.

'Beep! Brianswap/genius.2.idiot. Urgent. Find conversion files. Matter of life and shutdown.'

'Burp! Brianswap\idiot.2.genius,' came the reply. 'Who are you calling an idiot? Who wasted his time going to school? And who gave Ellie a thrashing and played games all day? Convert? Get lost!'

Mrs Thompson watched Brian open-mouthed. She reached for the telephone.

'Mrs Bossley? It's Susan Thompson at Rembrandt School.'

Hysterical cackles could be heard at the other end of the line. 'Can you come and fetch Brian? I think he has a virus . . . What do you mean, he'd be safer at school? No, I haven't got a sledge-hammer handy.' She put the phone down rather quickly.

'Mummy won't be long, dear . . . Or perhaps I should phone Daddy?'

When he got home, Brian tottered weakly towards the computer.

'System failure imminent,' he muttered. 'System failure imminent.'

But Mum got there first. She barred his way.

'Get away from it,' she shrieked. 'I've had enough of your jokes.'

She shoved a couple of paracetamol into his hand.

'Go and lie down. I'm phoning the help line . . .'

Brian sank down in the corner as she dialled.

'. . . Hello? Hello! Yes, it's me again . . . I can't access any files, and when I do, they've been changed. My deadline is Friday and my elves have been brutally murdered . . . Yes, I have got the right number . . . Wait, I haven't finished yet! The computer thinks I'm its mother and it wants me to play games . . . What? No, I am not on any medication.' She slammed the phone down. 'Where's the manual? I'm going to complain.'

She stormed out.

Brian dragged himself to his feet and sank down at the computer. He had to do it before she got back. He opened 'all abot me'. He could hear Mum throwing books about in the lounge. He scrolled down quickly to the end of the text. Then he heard Mum's footsteps. She was coming back. He deleted the last two lines and typed

`I want to be Brian again.`

Mum opened the door. Brian grabbed the mouse. He felt the bytes emptying down his arm and rushing back to the computer.

A prompt box suddenly came up on the screen.

`On your bike. I'm staying put . . .`

For a moment Brian thought he was going to pass out. But then the message slowly faded and a sloppy, bubbly feeling sloshed up into his brain as if he was being filled with lemonade.

He smiled.

'BRIAN!'

Mum leaped at him and tried to grab the mouse. An army of electronic ants seemed to march from the mouse, into her fingers, up her arm and finally into her skull.

Mum began skipping round the room. Brian watched her in amazement. She danced out into the kitchen. She picked up a tea-towel and tied it around her head like a scarf. Then she took a basket. She filled it with sandwiches, cake and a bottle of pop.

'What a lovely day for a picnic!' she chirped as she opened the back door. Then she seemed to change her mind. She laid down the basket and went over to the kitchen cupboard. She brought out a large wooden rolling-pin.

'Mum!' said Brian, 'What are you doing?'

'I'm going to sort out those pixies once and for all,' she muttered. 'And please call me Ellie.'

Faces
Dennis Hamley

The man ran desperately along the road. His heartbeats sounded in his ears in time with his echoing feet on the iron-hard, icy ground. Sweat poured into his eyes though the night was bitterly cold. The headlights of cars going the other way swept past him. No cars seemed to be going his way. His desperation grew.

At last, the sound of a car came from behind him. He stepped into the road and into the glare of its headlamps, waving his arms and hardly caring for his safety. The car drew to a halt and the man opened the passenger door.

'For God's sake take me to the next town,' he gasped.

The driver wore a heavy overcoat, a hat pulled low over his face and a woollen scarf.

'Certainly,' he said in a level, smooth, mellifluous* voice.

For some minutes the journey proceeded quietly. The muffled figure behind the wheel drove speedily along the straight, dark road. His new passenger regained his breath and some of his composure.

At length, the driver spoke. Once again there could be noticed the calm evenness in his voice.

'Tell me, sir – for indeed I could not help but notice the state you were in when I stopped for you – the cause of your perturbation.'*

The passenger gulped. For a moment it seemed as though he was unwilling to say anything about his experiences. Then – in the warm, steadily-driven car,

---

*mellifluous – sweet, pleasant
*perturbation – disturbance

insulated from the evils of the dark night outside – he relaxed.

'Very well,' he said.

'My own car broke down about three miles back along the road. I was unable to do anything without help. I realized I was miles from anywhere; no traffic seemed willing to stop for me. It seemed my only course was to walk until I found a house where I might either obtain help or make a telephone call.

'After walking for about half a mile, I saw a house standing back from the road. It was dark, thatched, ivy-covered – seemingly deserted. Nevertheless, it seemed worth enquiring there, in case it was inhabited. Therefore I went up to the front door and knocked at it. To my surprise, it was opened at once.

'In the darkness stood a person – I judged her to be a woman – holding a candle which revealed nothing of her but only the bare floorboards and walls of the entrance hall.

'"Come inside," she said to me.

'The woman beckoned to me and turned away. I followed her. A man's voice, in tones of sweet reasonableness, called from another room.

'"Who is it, my dear?"

'In an equally soft voice, the woman answered, "It is he whom we have expected."

'It was then that I should have run from that accursed place for ever. But I did not. For I felt thankful at having found shelter with people who sounded so pleasant, so kind.

'I was led into a room which once again was in darkness, lit only by faint moonlight which filtered in through curtainless, leaded windows. The shape of a man could be seen standing behind a table, placed on which I could just make out the outlines of an oil lamp. The woman moved away from me to stand beside him.

'For a moment, there was complete silence and stillness.

'Then the man leant forward. He lit the oil lamp. Its warm, yellow light threw leaping shadows around the room. I looked round at the features of the room now revealed – the beamed ceiling, the oak table, the heavy, carved chairs. Then I looked at my new companions, now that I had light to see them with.

'And then my face froze into horror and my voice formed itself into a wordless scream.

'For the faces of both the man and the woman were the same. No mouth. No nose. No eyes. They were smooth, bare, featureless – as eggs.

'Without thinking twice, I turned and ran – out of the house, onto the road, carrying on the way I had been going before; desperate for help, for consolation, for assurance that I had been merely the victim of a mistake, a practical joke, an hallucination, perhaps a nightmare.

'And then, as if in answer to a prayer, you stop for me and I am back in the world of normality.'

He settled back into the front seat of the car as it sped smoothly onward.

The driver's hand stayed calmly on the steering wheel. For the first time since the passenger had commenced his story, he spoke.

'You say their faces had no features on them: they were, in fact, quite blank?'

'Yes,' said the passenger.

The driver turned to his companion and with his left hand removed his scarf.

'You mean, like this?'

No mouth. No nose. No eyes. A face as blank and smooth and featureless as an egg.

Banana
Neil Arksey

On Titch Wilson's eleventh birthday, his grandparents had given him a chunky black divers' watch. It was exactly the type he had always wanted; he was over the moon. After a huge lunch followed by chocolate cake, he and his sister Lisa set off home across the common.

It was the end of the summer holidays and the grass on the common was all dried up and yellowy brown from countless days of brilliant, hot sunshine.

Shouting and swearing, charging around like headless chickens and angry rhinos, the boys from the neighbourhood were having a 'friendly' game. Clouds of dust swirled up from the ground as they pushed, barged and kicked each other and, occasionally, kicked the ball.

Titch stopped to watch.

The amazing Steve Bates was heading for the goal. Twisting – first this way, then that – he dodged effortlessly through half a dozen frenzied defenders. Still more ran to block his path, others were hot on his tail.

'On the wing, Batesy!' yelled Titch, suddenly spotting a slender shape down the far side, legging it like a maniac into open space. 'Out to the right!'

Others – on the pitch – shouted similar advice, but Batesy kept going. He side-stepped one player, skipped over the sliding tackle of another, and swerved to avoid head-on collision with a third.

Titch hurried along beside the action. 'Batesy!' he yelled, louder than anyone. 'On your RIGHT! Pass it out, you idiot. *Pass the ball!*'

Still Batesy kept going. It was impressive. He had gone round two more players and the goalie was coming out to tackle him. The lone winger had jogged to a standstill almost directly in front of the open goal.

'Call for it!' Titch screamed to him. And then: 'Batesy, you big dope, pass the blinking . . .'

Too late! Batesy was down – a fair tackle – and the ball was being passed, fast and furious, back the other way. Batesy's side had been caught short, heading in the wrong direction. Now the opposition were running through.

As Batesy scrambled to his feet, at the far end a player was already whacking it home. There were loud cheers and hung heads – it had been the deciding goal. The game was over. Batesy's side had lost.

Batesy looked less than pleased.

'You!' he snarled, charging over. '*You* have just cost us the game, you little . . .'

'*What!?!!*' Titch looked round for support. '*Ref . . . !*'

'Your shouting and insults distracted me.' Batesy was standing right up against him, towering over, a head taller. 'Your stupid loud mouth's too big for your stupid little body!' Batesy shoved him hard in the chest.

'Oi!' Lisa yelled from somewhere behind. Titch stood his ground.

'Come on, Batesy,' he said, 'I only offered advice.'

'*You?*' Batesy laughed. 'Offer *me* advice?'

Titch nodded.

'When you can play as good as me,' said Batesy, jabbing a finger in Titch's chest, 'you can *maybe* offer suggestions. Till then – *shut it*.' Shoving Titch once more, he turned and stormed off.

'If you can't accept advice,' shouted Titch to his back, 'you'll never improve. And if you can't take losing, you shouldn't play.' Batesy had stopped in his tracks. 'Anyway,' added Titch, 'I'm as good a player as you, in my own position – and you know it!'

Batesy turned. '*Yeah?*' he sneered.

'*Yeah!*' said Titch.

'Don't make me laugh!' said Batesy. 'There's only one of us gonna be picked for the Coppice First Team this term – that's me and *you* know it.'

'Rubbish!' said Titch.

''Snot!' said Batesy.

'Wanna bet?'

'How much?'

'Er . . .'

'Come on – how much?' repeated Batesy.

Titch couldn't think. He'd never actually made a proper bet. 'This watch,' he said.

Batesy grabbed his wrist, looked at the watch and smiled. 'Done!' he said, shaking his hand like he wanted to wrench it off. And then he was heading off across the common, laughing and joking with his mates.

'Why are boys so stupid?' said Lisa, punching Titch, hard, on the shoulder. 'You included,' she added. 'If you lose your watch, you're for it, *Mr Hothead*. And you never even got him to bet you something in return. Coppice is a much bigger school than Daybrook Primary, you know. There might be others there better than you.'

Titch shook his head. 'Not in goal,' he said. 'I'm the best.'

The first few days at Coppice Hill School were non-stop. Titch's head spun with all the new information – the layout of the classrooms and timetables, new subjects and teachers' names, school rules and routines. There were thirty new names and faces in his class – only six were familiar. There were four other classes in the same year.

Those who had been at Daybrook tended to come together at break. Batesy greeted him each time with a reminder about the bet.

'Hey – shrimp! Taking care of my watch? Looking forward to the trials?'

'You think you're such a big shot,' replied Titch, 'but which of us had the nerve to make the bet?'

Mr Drisco, the physics teacher, was in charge of the soccer team.

On the afternoon of the trials, boys gathered in the middle of the pitch. Mr Drisco marched out from the pavilion with his clipboard.

'Right!' he barked. 'When I call out your name, step forward and identify yourself. State what position you play, then stand in the appropriate line. Clear?'

Lines formed for each position. Hopeful strikers stood in the queue with Batesy, others lined up to be goalie, but the majority were going for midfield positions.

Titch's name was last on the register. When it was called, he stepped forward.

'Goalie, Sir!' he yelled.

Mr Drisco lowered his clipboard and peered over the top of his glasses, as if searching for the owner of this voice. Finally, focusing on Titch, he said sternly, 'You're pulling my leg, aren't you, Wilson?'

Laughter spread through the lines. Batesy's was, of course, by far the loudest.

'No, Sir,' said Titch. 'Goalkeeping is what I'm good at . . . Sir.'

'Well, a simple test should settle this,' said Mr Drisco. 'Goalies-to-be, follow me!'

There were seven other boys – three couldn't touch him, Titch knew for sure. He'd have to see about the rest.

'Right!' said Mr Drisco as they reached the goal posts. 'You are all going to jump for the crossbar. If you don't reach it straight away – keep trying. When you're ready . . .'

Titch froze. He knew he couldn't reach the crossbar. The others were jumping and Mr Drisco was staring at him, one eyebrow raised, as if to say, 'Well? What are we waiting for?' There was nothing else for it. He jumped.

'OK, OK – that's enough!' said Mr Drisco after a couple of minutes. 'Anybody, apart from Wilson, fail to make contact?' Too out of breath to speak, they all shook their heads. 'Very good,' said Mr Drisco. 'Wait here by the goal. Wilson, I suggest you join a line for another position.'

'But, Sir . . .' pleaded Titch, jogging to keep up with Mr Drisco. 'Sir, that's not fair . . .'

'Excellent jumps, Wilson, *for your height* . . .'

'Sir, I'm better than . . .'

Mr Drisco silenced him with a stare. 'You're too short,' he snapped, 'it's as simple as that. I'm not having someone goalkeeping for the team if they can't reach the crossbar.'

They had arrived back at the lines of boys. Batesy had a huge grin on his face, others were tittering. Titch had never felt so terrible.

Though he tried for a couple of other positions, of course he didn't have a chance. He had always played in goal – his skills were with his hands and body, not his feet. He could dive, he could catch and fist, he could even kick a ball, but when he tried to dribble or tackle, his feet got tangled up.

'So – how will you explain the missing watch?' said Lisa, as they walked home from school. 'Gran and Grandad will be heartbroken. Mum will *murder* you.'

'He's not getting it,' said Titch. 'The bet's not over till this term's finished. I watched the penalty shoot-out – the remaining goalies may all have been bigger than me, but they were rubbish. Sooner or later, Drisco will *have* to try me.'

Titch was a born goalie, he was a natural. His mum was forever complaining about how he couldn't sit still like ordinary people. He leapt around, throwing himself across the floor and diving for imaginary balls, even when watching the telly. His reflexes were second to none, his handling skills were excellent, his strength and speed – good as the best. The one thing he lacked was *height*.

This wasn't news to Titch – after all, everyone did call him 'Titch'. But it had never been a problem before – there had never been a crossbar. It had always been two posts, or two jackets on the ground, and if somebody kicked the ball above the goalie's reach, it didn't count. He'd always worked hard on getting extra lift, he could jump very high for his height. But not, according to Mr Drisco, high enough.

It had only been a matter of a few centimetres, certainly no more than six – Titch was sure he could soon gain that much. He started eating as much protein, fresh vegetables and fruit as he could. Chicken or egg sandwiches for lunch, fish or meat and vegetables for supper and, when his mum allowed it, he even ate cold leftovers – fish fingers or whatever – for breakfast. He cut down on the sweets, crisps and fizzy drinks, but drank more milk for his bones.

Every morning and evening he climbed onto a chair and hung from the top of the door-frame, letting himself stretch till his fingers hurt too much to bear. He did rope-skipping every day to increase his bounce, and swam as often as he could, because someone had told him it lengthened growing limbs. And, of course, he still practised his goalkeeping.

Batesy, meanwhile, was becoming less cocky with his mocking. Though the First Team had won at the start of term, it had not happened again. Plenty of goals were being scored by the forwards, but even more were being let in by the goalie. It was only a matter of time now. Mr Drisco, Titch felt sure, must soon offer him a trial.

But each week when, at the end of the physics lesson, Titch asked Mr Drisco if he could try for the First Team, the reply was the same:

'When you can reach the crossbar, Wilson, you'll have your chance.'

'But, Sir . . .'

'Wilson – I'm a physics teacher, a scientist, a man of reason . . . *till provoked*. Can you reach the crossbar?'

'No, Sir.'

'Then *cease*!'

Every day, walking home past the football pitch, Titch jumped for the crossbar. Lisa checked for any progress. The results were less than promising.

By halfway through the term, however, the First Team's results were less than promising too. They couldn't even manage a draw. Mr Drisco had tried playing the reserve goalie with no improvement in results.

When Titch once again made his plea to be considered for the team, Mr Drisco didn't take it too well.

'Wilson – you ask the same question every week. Every week I give the same reply. I think your mind must be too much on football and not enough on physics.' Titch bowed his head. 'Next week, Wilson, in front of the class, you will explain, using diagrams drawn on the blackboard, the solution to tonight's homework – exercise C. I want to see whether you *are* capable of logical thought.'

Everyone turned to look at Titch.

'*In front of the class*, Sir?'

'Correct.'

'But, Sir . . .'

'*WILSON!*'

That was that.

Though he was a bit of a kidder, Titch was not the sort that enjoyed getting up in front of people and doing something *serious*. He dreaded the thought of being laughed at and tended to make a mess of such situations.

Every night that week, instead of his usual training and goalkeeping practice, he sat at home struggling with the physics homework.

Lisa was shocked. 'What's come over you?' she said. 'You're never normally this quiet or still. It's really quite nice.'

But Titch was too busy working to reply.

The last night before it was due, he stayed up late checking and rechecking his work. At midnight, he leapt into bed, set the alarm and turned out the light. But, with his head full of circles and lines from his homework diagrams, he couldn't get to sleep. For a whole week he'd thought about nothing else. But now he was confident about doing those diagrams on the board tomorrow, old feelings of frustration about not being in the First Team began, once again, to nag.

Suddenly, he had a brainwave.

To reach the blackboard, he had to stand on tiptoe.

Having drawn two vertical lines, Titch joined them together at the top with a horizontal. Beneath he drew a circle and wrote: 'diameter – approx thirty centimetres'.

The class began to murmur and titter.

'Silence!' yelled Mr Drisco.

To the side of the circle, Titch drew a pin man with arms reaching up, the hands just a few centimetres below the horizontal line. The diagram was finished. Smiling with satisfaction, he turned to face the class. Mr Drisco was frowning, everyone else grinning.

Mr Drisco waved the sheet of homework questions and pointed at the blackboard. 'What,' he bellowed, 'is *that* a proof of, Wilson?'

'Sir, I've done all the homework problems,' said Titch, holding up his exercise book, 'but after I finished them, I came up with a proof of something else.'

Faces turned to see Drisco's reaction. 'Explain yourself!' he barked. 'Explain your diagram!'

'Well, Sir,' said Titch, gesturing at the board, 'as you can see – since a football . . .' he pointed to the circle '. . . is about thirty centimetres wide, a goalie . . .' here he pointed to his pin man '. . . does *not* need to be able to jump all the way to the crossbar in order to stop it. A goalie only needs to reach as high as fifteen centimetres below the crossbar in order to be able to stop *any* shot.'

You could have heard a pin drop.

You could have heard an ant sneeze (if ants had noses).

Mr Drisco scratched his head and stared at the diagram on the blackboard. 'Wilson,' he said, after a very long moment, '. . . would you be interested in trying for the First Eleven?'

The class exploded.

It was penalty shoot-out time again. Quite a crowd had gathered on the playing field to watch. Five players had been selected from the First Team, they were to take shots against each of three goalies: the main, the reserve and Titch. Batesy, one of the five, was arguing and shouting with the others in the centre of the pitch.

'You can't win, Batesy!' yelled Titch, from the goal. 'If I'm chosen for the team, you lose the bet. If I'm not, the team is doomed.' Batesy scowled and spat at the ground. 'But don't worry,' added Titch, 'I'm not letting *any* get past me!'

After the first three players had done their worst, Titch was smiling. Behind the goal, Mr Drisco was looking pleasantly surprised. Each of the other goalies had let in two, but he, Titch Wilson, had saved all three. If he saved the next one, he'd be in the team.

Walking out towards the penalty spot, Batesy looked ready to kill.

'This is it!' yelled Titch. 'Just you and me.'

Stony-faced, Batesy placed the ball on the ground and paced backwards ten wide steps.

The crowd grew hushed.

Shaking his arms and legs one last time for looseness, Titch crouched low and focused his whole attention on the ball.

With a little skipping movement, Batesy began his run.

He was coming.

Faster and faster.

'*Grrrrrrrrrrr!*'

He was growling.

Louder and louder.

He was *charging*.

As the outside edge of Batesy's boot made contact with the ball, suddenly everything seemed to slip into slow motion. It was like an action replay. Titch heard himself thinking, *It's a BANANA!* And sure enough, the ball curved up and out before, gradually, as if pulled by some special force, it began to curl back. The ball was homing in on the top right corner of the goal.

Titch sprung, soared and – *yes!* – fisted the ball clear.

Jumping and cheering, the crowd swarmed towards the goal.

But what was this? He was still in the air! He could hardly believe it. *He was hanging from the crossbar!* And there, in the mob below, was Lisa – waving her arms, grinning and shouting. Mr Drisco and Batesy were pushing their way through.

'Very impressive!' yelled Mr Drisco.

Batesy looked up at Titch. 'Yeah,' he said grudgingly, '*very* impressive.' He held out his hand. 'But I bet you can't do *that* again.'

'Luckily, to save goals he doesn't need to,' said Mr Drisco. 'He's *proved* that.'

Titch dropped to the ground and grabbed Batesy's hand. 'No more bets,' he said. 'But we should shake hands as teammates.'

Batesy looked like he was trying to decide whether to snap Titch's elbow or yank his arm from its socket. His eyes, lingering on Titch's divers' watch, seemed suddenly to notice Mr Drisco's watchful gaze. 'OK, then,' he said, managing the slightest smile, '. . . as teammates.'

Titch grinned.

And they shook.

The Bakerloo Flea
Michael Rosen

Not long ago I was in a pub round the Elephant and Castle, and I got talking to a woman, an oldish woman. And we were talking about this and that, and she said she used to be a cleaner down the Underground. I didn't know, but it seems as if every night after the last tube, they switch the electric current off and teams of night-cleaners go through the Underground, along the tunnels, cleaning up all the muck, rubbish, fag-ends and stuff that we chuck onto the lines. They sweep out between the lines on one station, and then, in a gang of about six or seven, walk on to the next station along the lines in the tunnels.

Anyway this woman (I don't know her name), she says to me:

'Did you ever hear talk of the Bakerloo flea?'

'Bakerloo flea?' I said. 'No, no never.'

'Well,' she said, 'you know there are rats down there – down the Underground? Hundreds of 'em. And the thing is,' she said, 'is that some of them have grown enormous. Huge great big things.'

'I've heard of them,' I said. 'Super rats.'

'Right,' she says. 'Now you tell me,' she says, 'what lives on rats? Fleas, right? Fleas. So – the bigger the rats the bigger the fleas. Stands to reason. These rats, they feed on all the old garbage that people throw down on the lines. It's amazing what people throw away, you know.'

She told me, they found a steak down there once, lipstick, a bowler hat, beads, a box of eggs and hundreds and hundreds of sweets – especially Maltesers and those balls of bubble gum you get out of slot machines.

Anyway, the rats eat these, get big, and it seems that one day they were working the Bakerloo Line – Elephant and Castle to Finchley Road – and just before Baker Street one of the women in the gang was looking ahead, and she screamed out:

'Look – look – what's that?' Up in front was a great, grey, spiky thing with huge hairy legs and big jaws. It was as big as a big dog – bigger.

And the moment she screamed, it jumped away from them, making a sort of grating, scraping noise. Well, they were scared stiff. Scared stiff. But they had to finish the job, so they carried on up the line to Finchley Road. But they didn't see it again that night or the next, or the next.

Some of them thought they'd imagined it, because it can get very spooky down there. They sing and shout a lot she told me, and tell saucy jokes, not fit for my ears.

Anyway, about a fortnight later, at the same place – just before Baker Street on the Bakerloo Line – suddenly one of them looks up and there it was again. A great, big, grey, spiky thing with long legs and big jaws.

'It's a flea, sure to God it's a flea,' one of them said.

The moment it heard this, again it jumped. Again, they heard this scraping, grating sound, and it disappeared down the tunnel – in the dark. They walked on, Baker Street, St John's Wood, Swiss Cottage, to Finchley Road. Nothing.

Anyway – this time they had a meeting. They decided it *was* a flea, a gigantic flea, and it must have grown up from a family of fleas that had lived for years and years growing bigger and bigger, sucking the blood of all the fat rats down there.

So they decided that it was time to tell one of the high-ups in London Transport, or they wouldn't go down there any more.

For a start off, no one'd believe them.

'Just a gang of women seeing things in the dark,' the supervisor said.

Right! One of them had a bright idea. She said:

'I'll tell you what we'll do – we'll tell them that we're coming out on strike, and we'll tell the papers about the flea, the Bakerloo flea. It'll be a huge scandal – no one'll dare go by tube, it'll be a national scandal.'

So they threatened the manager with this, and this time the high-ups really moved. They were so scared the story might get out, and they'd be blamed, and one of *them* would lose their jobs.

So for a start they stopped all cleaning on the Bakerloo Line, and one of the high-ups went down the tunnel with the women. You can just see it, can't you? Four in the morning, a gang of six women with feather dusters, and one of the bowler hat and briefcase brigade walking down the tunnel on the hunt for the Bakerloo flea. Sounded incredible to me.

Anyway, it seems as if they came round that same corner just before Baker Street and the women had gone quiet and the bloke was saying: 'If this is a hoax, if this is a trick . . . ' when they heard that awful, hollow, scraping noise.

At first they couldn't see it, but then – there it was – not *between* the lines this time – *on* the lines – a gigantic flea. No question, that's what it was.

Well, he took one look at it, and next moment he was backing off.

'Back, ladies, back. Back, ladies!'

Of course *he* was more scared than *they* were. Terrified. But he was even more terrified when one of the women let out this scream. Not because *she* was scared, but to scare off the flea. And it worked. It jumped. Right out of sight.

Well, there was no carrying on up the line that night.

'Back, ladies, back,' was all he could say, and back they went.

Next thing they knew, they were all called into an office with a carpet and the Queen on the wall. And there was a whole gang of these men.

First thing, one of them says, they weren't to let anyone know of this, no one at all must ever hear of what they had all seen. There was no point in letting a panic develop. Anyway, next he says: 'We haven't let the grass grow under our feet. We've got a scientist with us.'

And then the scientist, he says:

'I've got this powder. Deadly flea powder. All you need to do is spread this up and down the Bakerloo Line, and there'll be no more trouble with this flea thing.'

Well, the woman in the pub – I never found out her name – said:

'So who's going to spread this stuff about down there? The Army?'

'No,' the man said. 'We don't see any need for that. You,' he says, 'you.'

'So that's a fine one,' the woman said to me. 'First of all they said it was just a bunch of women afraid of the dark, then they send Tarzan in pinstripes down there and he can't get out fast enough, and now it's us that has to spread this flea powder.'

'Well,' she said, 'we knew it wouldn't be any good anyway. Flea powder never is.'

They took it down there, threw it about between Regent's Park and Baker Street and Swiss Cottage – while up above, in the big houses, ambassadors from all over the world slept soundly in their beds. They told them not to go down for a week, and not to breathe a word of it to anyone.

'They were more scared of a story in the papers than we were of the flea,' she said.

It hadn't attacked anyone, no one had seen it there in day time, so down they went. But there it was again – sitting there just before Baker Street, with some of the powder sticking to the hairs on its legs. But this time, instead of hopping away down the line, it turned and faced them. They turned and ran, and then it leaped. It leaped at the women, and they ran back down the tunnel to Regent's Park. This great, grey flea was trying to get at them.

'We screamed,' she said, 'we really screamed, but it was after us, 'cos you see that damned flea powder hadn't killed the flea – it had killed the rats. It was starving for fresh blood. Probably *mad* for blood, by now,' she said. 'We ran and ran and the flea was hopping – but it was hitting the roof of the tunnel, it was so mad to get at us. There was this terrible scraping sound of its shell on the roof of the tunnel, and it'd fall back onto the lines. So we could move faster than it. We rushed back to Regent's Park, and calls went up and down the line and all over the system to lock the gates on every station and seal the system. Seal off the Underground system of London. Well, it was about four o'clock – two hours to go before a million people would be down there.

'What were they going to do? Upstairs in the office they were in a blind panic. They could've done something about it earlier, instead of fobbing us off. They couldn't call in the Army without telling the Minister, and if they told the Minister, he'd tell the Prime Minister, and all the high-ups would get the sack. So they had this plan to turn the current on, and run the maintenance train at high speed through the tunnel from Finchley Road to the Elephant and Castle, in the hope that it would get killed beneath the wheels of the train, or smashed against the buffers at the Elephant.

'They did it. They sent it through. Of course *that* didn't work. We knew it wouldn't work. Anyone that's lived with a flea knows you can't squash fleas – you've got to crack 'em. They're hard, rock hard.

'After the maintenance man ran the maintenance train through, they went down to the gates at Regent's Park, and they stood and listened, and from down below they could hear the grating, scraping noise of its shell on its legs. Of course, it was obvious now why it had stuck to this stretch of the line all the time. Some of the juiciest rubbish was in the bins round those posh parts, so you got the biggest rats, so that was where you got the great Bakerloo flea.

'So now they had less than two hours to get rid of the flea, or leave it for a day and run the risk of letting a million people down into the tunnels to face a flea, starving, starving for blood, or shutting the whole system down and telling everyone to go by bus.

'Well you know what happened?' she said. 'We did it. We got rid of it.'

'You did?'

'Yes, we did it. Vera's old man worked on the dustcarts for Camden Council. She knew how to kill the flea. It was Vera's plan that what we'd do was go down, actually down onto the line at Oxford Circus with dustbin lids, banging them with brushes and broom handles, and drive the flea back up the line to Finchley Road where the Bakerloo Line comes out of the tunnel into the open air. And at Finchley Road, Vera's old man and his gang would have a couple of carts backed up into the tunnel. And that's what we did. We got driven to Vera's place to get her old man up, on to his mates' places to get them up, then they went to the Council builder's yard to get boards, builders' planks. We got the lids of the bins, and down we went. Oxford Circus, Regent's Park, Baker Street, St John's

Wood, Swiss Cottage, Finchley Road, and we shouted and we banged, and we banged and we shouted every step of the way.

'We saw it just once at Swiss Cottage waiting for us, but we walked together holding the lids up in front of us like shields, and it was as if it knew it couldn't get at us this time, 'cos it turned – it had just room to turn in the tunnel – and as we came up to Finchley Road still banging and shouting, it leaped – not at us, but at one of the carts. Alongside it was the other one, between the wheels were the boards, some of them stacked up to block off all the gaps. The flea was trapped between us with our lids and the back of the dustcarts. It leaped, it hit the roof of the tunnel, just like it did when it chased us. We shouted and banged. It leaped again. This time we had it. It was in the back of the dustcart.

'We kept up the banging and the shouting. We got as near to the back of the dustcart as we could. We could see it there, every hair of its legs, and Vera shouts:

'"Turn it on, Bob, turn it on," and Bob turned on the masher (they call it 'The Shark') in the back of his cart. And it bit into the back of the flea like giant nails crunching through eggshells. The smell was revolting. Bit by bit, the flea was dragged into the cart. We could see it as it went: first its body, then its legs. I'll never forget the sight of those huge hairy legs twitching about in the back of Bob's cart, Vera shouting:

'"You've got him, love, you've got him!"

'He had, too. That was that. That was the end of the Bakerloo flea. But do you know, when we got up to the top, that load from head office were there. They were crying, crying out of relief, crying their eyes out. Twenty minutes later, hundreds and thousands of people were down there, off to work, none the wiser. They didn't know about any flea, any Bakerloo flea. They don't even know we go down there every night cleaning up their mess for them. Of course, head office made us promise never to breathe a word of it. We promised.

'Vera said: "What's it worth to you?"

'He said: "Your honour. Your word. And your word's your honour."

'And they gave us a week's extra holiday tagged on to August Bank Holiday that year.'

She told me I was the first person she'd ever told the story to, and told me never to tell anyone. The scandal would be terrible. I don't know whether to believe her or not.

Star Pupil
Lorna Read

'Remember the day Spike started in our class?' I said to the gang the other day. It was one of our Spike Reminiscence Sessions. We'd talked about him a lot since he'd gone – to keep his memory alive, I suppose. 'Mr Williams said he came from a tiny island off the coast of Australia –'

'– and when he asked us to look it up in Geography, it wasn't there!' Tony interrupted.

'Do you think Mr Williams was in on it?' asked Yasmin, in her soft, husky voice.

I shook my head. 'No. He couldn't have been. It was part of Spike's test that nobody should find out.'

'Yes, you're right, Lee,' Tony said. 'So he can't have known. But surely, anyone could tell from looking at him that he wasn't like someone from an Australian island. They wouldn't have purple hair, for a start, would they?'

'Or strange bits of metal jewellery in the middle of their ears,' Joe said.

'Maybe he hypnotized the Head and Mr Williams,' I said.

'Maybe he hypnotized all of us,' Tony added.

'Especially me,' Yasmin said wistfully. Her friend Kerry put an arm around her.

One thing we were all in agreement about was that we missed him like crazy. Without Spike in our school, classes were dull, dinner-times were dead and our computers seemed to plod along like hippopotamuses.

Yet, on the first day that he joined us, we just thought he was a hopeless weirdo . . .

*

'This is Spike,' Mr Williams said. 'Say hello to him, class.'

'Hello, Spike,' we all repeated mechanically. Our brains were whirring, trying to classify him. Was he a punk, a goth, a piercing freak? He didn't look as though he got much sun. His skin was a kind of greenish grey, as if he were about to be sick.

I moved my chair a few inches to the right as Spike was put to sit at the spare desk on my left. Soon, we were deep into our history lesson about Ancient Rome, a period which really fires my imagination. I was out there with the legion, dressed in creaking leather and a heavy battle helmet, carrying the standard.

Suddenly, a sharp, slightly squeaky voice spoke into my left ear. 'I see you have a mental video chip. Very advanced,' he said.

I shot a look at Spike and frowned. 'Ssh, we're not allowed to talk in class,' I whispered.

Mr Williams gave us one of his threatening looks, to press my point home.

At break-time, we all formed into our usual clusters of friends. Spike wandered off on his own. Everyone stared at him as he walked round the borders of the playground, examining plants and trees.

He looked so lonely that I felt sorry for him and went off to rescue him.

'Come on. I'll introduce you to my friends,' I offered.

I could see all the other kids staring as Spike and I walked across the yard together.

Tony, Joe, Yasmin and Kerry introduced themselves.

'Don't look so scared. Smile!' I said.

'What is "smile"?' asked Spike.

'This.' I stretched the corners of my mouth out in a grin. Everybody laughed. 'It means you feel friendly, or happy,' I explained.

Spike looked puzzled.

'When you like someone, you smile at them,' I expanded.

Spike's thin lips suddenly formed the widest grin imaginable. I thought his ears were going to shoot off the side of his head.

Kerry glanced at her watch. 'That's funny,' she said. 'My watch says half past four. Time to go home, folks, and we haven't had lunch yet!'

'Mine says midnight,' said Tony.

'Mine seems to have stopped,' I discovered.

None of us knew why. Not then, but we did later, of course. Right then, we were happy to have a much longer morning break than usual, because the teacher's watch had stopped, too.

I'll never forget that first school dinner with Spike. Some kids brought sandwiches, but not our gang. We always went for the hot meal, especially if there was jam roly-poly or fly cemetery pie for afters.

Spike watched us closely and put various things on his tray. We all watched, appalled, as he dumped his custard tart on top of his roast chicken, then poured gravy over the lot.

'You're never going to *eat* that?' Tony asked in horror, as Spike picked up a spoon and began to tuck in.

'Very nice!' Spike said, and smiled that face-splitting smile again while we all felt ill.

On subsequent days, we tried to educate him in what went with what, but he continued to mix everything up together, insisting it tasted much nicer like that. Ugh!

That afternoon, we had an art lesson where we did designs on computers. We were learning how to lay out the pages of a newspaper.

No sooner had I switched mine on than a Roman legion marched across the screen.

'Hey, that looks like me!' I exclaimed, pointing at a red-haired captain carrying a standard with an eagle painted on it. 'Where did Mr Clark find this brilliant program?'

Then I noticed that everyone had different things on their machines. Yasmin was gazing at herself dressed in tiny shorts and a cut-off top singing into a microphone on stage in front of a huge audience. Tony was driving a racing car, his brow knitted in concentration as he roared past his rival and took the lead. Kerry lazed in a hammock beside a still blue sea.

Then Mr Clark started speaking and next time I looked, Romans, sea, racing circuit and stage had all vanished and we were each faced with a boring page layout.

I was amazed at Spike's computer skills. He seemed to be able to do exactly what Mr Clark asked, without even touching the mouse or the keyboard, while the rest of us struggled as we tried to change our typefaces.

At some point, Spike seemed to get cheesed off. He sat there with his arms folded and suddenly his computer began to make the rudest noises. People started to giggle.

'Whoever's doing that, please stop, it isn't funny,' scolded Mr Clark.

The noises went on. 'Detention!' warned Mr Clark.

'It's Spike's computer,' I said. 'It's gone on the blink!'

We all roared as Clarky stood over it with a baffled expression, pressing buttons, while the computer continued to blow big fat raspberries at him. Then the bell went and we all switched our machines off. Spike's blew one last, loudest raspberry before the screen went blank – and just before it did, I felt sure I caught a glimpse of Spike's own face on the screen, pulling tongues. And you know what? His tongue was purple.

*

Friday afternoon we had a double Geography period. Mr Williams took the globe out of the cupboard. Then he picked on Spike.

'Please show the class where Goolygong Island is,' he said. 'That is the name of the place you come from, isn't it?'

A faint green flush crept over Spike's face as he twirled the glove, then jabbed his finger somewhere.

'That's not Australia, that's the Antilles Islands,' Mr Williams said. 'Surely you know where Australia is? Oh, never mind, sit down. Get your atlases out, class, and look for Goolygong.'

It wasn't there.

'Stand up, Spike.' Spike shot me a desperate look as Mr Williams rapped out his order. 'Where exactly *do* you come from?'

I saw Spike give a big gulp. His voice came out all high and squeaky. 'I come from a distant planet called Karn, in a galaxy called Philodendron 23.'

'I suppose you want me to take the star map out of the cupboard now,' said Mr Williams sarcastically. 'I'm giving you lines for being cheeky and disrupting the class. Write out one hundred times, by tomorrow, the name of every Melanesian island.'

The rest of us drew in our breath at the nastiness of this task, but Spike seemed unfazed. The lesson went on. Just before it was over, Spike put a blank piece of paper on his desk and went into a kind of trance, twiddling one of his ear ornaments. Then he stared at the paper. Suddenly, it was covered in neat lines. Each line consisted of a list of names: Malakula, San Cristóbal, Malaita . . .

'How did you do that, Spike?' I demanded, the moment the lesson was over and we were free to go home for the weekend.

'Do what?' he answered innocently.

'Do your lines without writing them. Have you got a mini-computer hidden away somewhere?'

'Maybe,' Spike said annoyingly.

'Where do you live, anyway?' I asked him.

'Oh . . . around,' he replied vaguely.

I gave up. 'Coming to the match tomorrow?' The rest of the gang were going to support our team.

'Okay. I'll come,' he agreed.

It wasn't a good day for our school. Midway through the second half, the other team were leading, two goals to nil. Then we all groaned as their star performer lobbed a vicious ball towards the centre of our goal. Our goalie didn't stand a chance.

None of us felt the sudden gust of wind that seemed to grab the ball in mid-air and make it change direction. It was as if that hurtling ball became a boomerang, zooming back where it had come from and sending the guy who'd kicked it crashing to the ground. One of our players just touched it with his toe and the ball took off in a graceful arc, spun high over the field like a UFO, and lobbed itself gently into the back of the opposing net. Two-one!

We all went mad, while the other team seemed completely rattled. After that, nothing could go right for them and we won six-two!

I hugged Spike, who was standing next to me. 'What a brilliant stroke of luck, the wind getting up just then,' I said joyfully.

He grinned from ear to ear. I still hadn't twigged. I think I must be really thick.

It was the incident with the goldfish that made me realize. Goldie had been a member of our class for some time. Different people undertook feeding and bowl-cleaning duties. The week after the match, it was my turn.

Spike stood watching me as I scooped the fish into a jam jar so I could scrub the algae off the side of the bowl and change the water.

'Goldfish are really boring. They never do anything but swim round and round,' I complained as I tipped her back into her sparkling clean bowl.

'What would you like the fish to do?' Spike asked.

'Dance,' I said and Yasmin giggled.

The fish danced. Up and down, round and round, in waltz time, then quicker, in a salsa rhythm. Yasmin and I gaped in amazement.

'Now what?' asked Spike.

I forced my lower jaw to meet my upper one again. 'Er . . . jump out of the bowl and loop the loop,' I said daftly.

Spike stared at the bowl. Suddenly, Goldie gave the most enormous leap.

'Oh no, she's going to die!' shrieked Yasmin.

But she didn't. She executed three full loops, then flopped gently back into the water. I gave her half a dozen ants' eggs as a reward.

'Spike, did you do that?' I asked suspiciously.

His face went completely expressionless.

'Are you really from a planet called Karn?' I pressed, feeling like an interrogator minus the blinding lamp and thumbscrews.

Spike looked round. Only Yasmin and I were in the room, the rest having gone outdoors for break. 'Yes,' he said. 'On the level. Cross my heart and hope to die.'

'Wow!' said Yasmin. 'How did you get here?'

'Our spacecraft are invisible to your eyes. I was delivered.'

'Why did you come here?' Yasmin asked.

'My final exams. I'm doing Interplanetary Studies. We each have to choose an inhabited planet and go there to learn about the people. But one of the most important things is that we must pass as one of you and not be discovered.'

'Then why did you tell Mr Williams you came from Karn?' asked Yasmin.

'It is very difficult for Karnians to tell a lie.'

'Okay,' I said, managing to get a word in before Yasmin. 'Did you make the football change course?'

'Yes.'

'And the goldfish dance? And put the pictures on the computer screens?'

'Yes. I just read your fantasies. In Karn, we have very strong mental powers. We have almost lost the power of speech. I had to have a special speech chip put in my throat before I came here,' Spike said.

'Those metal things. They're not just jewellery, are they?' asked Yasmin.

'No, I use them to communicate with my planet. This one here's a bit like your fax machines, and this one . . .' He explained each one in turn, while we marvelled.

'What else have you got to do while you're here?' I asked him.

'There's something very important that I *mustn't* do,' said Spike, after he'd told us fascinating things about his own school, and about his planet. 'I had to sign a solemn pledge to say that I wouldn't in any way interfere with the course of natural events on my host planet.'

We weren't quite sure what that meant. Perhaps it was something to do with evolution.

'And I mustn't show off my powers,' he said.

'It's a bit late for that!' I pointed out.

Spike's tricks didn't stop after that, but they got funnier and more subtle. Nobody outside our gang believed he came from Karn. They just thought he made up good stories. And as soon as he stopped letting himself come top in every test, his popularity increased. Soon, there was an outbreak of purple hair dye in the school. The diehard Spike fans started copying his dinners, eating chicken and custard pie with faces almost as green as his, and declaring that they loved it.

At the end of term, we had our Sports Day. One thing our school specialized in was the High Jump. Yasmin loved it, and so she and I positioned ourselves as close to the jump as possible, so we could watch the twisty-twiny way the jumpers wiggled over the pole.

While all kinds of other events went on around us, we watched the next jumper limber up. He was a big, muscular sixth-former and he took a ginormous leap, but got it wrong somehow and crashed into one of the posts supporting the jump.

It all happened so quickly. One moment Yasmin was standing beside me, the next, she was down on the ground, struck on the head by the toppling post. I lifted it off her. It wasn't that heavy.

'She's not breathing!' someone shouted.

Her face was as grey as Spike's.

'Stand back!' ordered a teacher. The Red Cross people came rushing over with their first aid kit, but there was nothing anybody could do. The post had struck her a direct blow on the temple. Yasmin was dead.

I felt myself crumple. I sank to the floor, and cried like a baby. Tony and Joe, who were just as stunned, tried to pick me up. A silent circle formed round Yasmin's body. Then Spike stepped forward. He knelt down and placed his hand on Yasmin's forehead. Nobody did a thing to stop him. We saw her eyes flicker, then open. Spike removed his hand and she sat up.

'What happened?' she asked, seeing the consternation written on faces all around her.

'You're alive!' I yelled, wanting to hug her, but I was held back as she was made to climb onto a stretcher, to be taken to hospital. I looked for Spike, but he'd vanished.

Next day, Yasmin was back in class, but Spike wasn't. There was no explanation. He had simply disappeared – off the face of the earth!

That's when life and school got dead boring. All the gang moped, especially Yasmin.

'He saved my life!' she kept saying. 'I never got a chance to thank him.'

The common opinion in school was that he'd disappeared because of the media attention. First, the local press and TV, then the nationals, got wind of the story. Newspapers offered the school vast sums of money for delivering Spike up so that he could be interviewed. One paper even referred to 'alien powers'. He would have been in danger of having his cover completely blown.

'I don't think we'll see him again, ever,' I told a sad Yasmin. 'But it was great knowing him, wasn't it?'

The summer vacation started off wet. I slumped around at home, thinking what fun it would be to have Spike around, making our dog dance and do crazy things.

One afternoon, I was in Dad's home office watching the rain batter against the window, when the fax machine whirred into life and out spilled a fax. I read it upside down as it snaked out of the machine, my heart bumping in excitement.

Karn Matriculation Board, Interplanetary Studies.
Report on Spikemarnio L. Kalendreth
1) Ability to pass physically as an Earthling: Fail.
His colour adjustment was imperfect.

2) *Success at controlling telekinetic powers: Fail. Spikemarnio used Karnian powers to show off and make himself popular.*

3) *Success at hiding Karnian identity: Fail. Spikemarnio's Truth chip revealed that he had told his Earthling class he was from Karn.*

I read right through the report: fail, fail, fail. The only subject to have gained a Pass was: *Sensitivity and compassion for alien life forms*.

Right at the end was a general summing-up:

Spikemarnio broke Karn Rule 1 in bringing a dead Earthling back to life. In so doing, he disrupted the natural course of events on Earth, but at the same time it shows him to have a natural inclination towards conservation, and an empathy for all life forms.

I stood with the torn-off fax in my hand, my heart heavy. Poor Spike, I thought. I hope he won't be punished.

Then the fax machine whirred again.

Hi, Lee! Shoved all this in the Omni-Translator. Hope it comes out okay. Know what it means? I've got to sit my Interplanetary Studies exam again. See you all next term!

Needle
Alan Gibbons

Needle, that's what it's all about.

Tonight I'm boxing against St George's. My first time in a proper show. Three one-and-a-half-minute rounds, and a belly full of butterflies. My first organized bout, but not my first fight. I know all about fighting. Boy, do I know about fighting!

It all started when me and Mum moved to Liverpool. What's wrong with that, I hear you say. I'll tell you what. I'm a Manc. That's right, Manchester born-and-bred. A Manchester United fan to boot. So what does my mum do? She takes me to live in Liverpool. People always say there's a rivalry between the two cities. Rivalry – that's one word for it!

Needle, that's what it's about.

I tell you, I was crying when she told me.

'But you can't!' I cried. 'All my mates are here.'

'Sorry, love,' said Mum. 'But it's the only way. We're going to live with your nan.'

In Liverpool. *Liverpool*. Oh, why did Mum and Dad have to split up?

'But Scousers hate Manchester people,' I cried.

'I'm a Scouser,' said Mum, smiling. 'And I don't hate you.'

'No,' I murmured. But Mum didn't count. Thirteen years she'd lived in Manchester, and in my eyes that made her an adopted Manc. Besides, she was my mum.

'But . . .' I stammered.

It was no use. Her mind was made up. A fortnight later I was walking into Stanley Comprehensive, clutching my school bag in one hand and my sinking heart in the other.

Which is when I ran into Chris Doherty, a professional Scouser but a pretty amateur human being.

'You new?' he asked.

'Yes.'

'What's your name?' he asked.

'Terry Keown.'

'Not from Liverpool, are you?' he asked. 'You talk like you've got a mouth full of cardboard.'

My heart's doing this rave dance in my rib cage. *Boom-badda-boom*.

'No.'

'Where then?'

'M–m–m . . .'

I saw his mates moving towards me.

'Madagascar?' he sneered, scenting blood.

'Mongolia?' demanded one of the other boys.

'No,' I said, my voice shrinking down to this strangled moan. 'Manchester.'

'You're a Manc!'

'Yes.'

'Who do you support?'

Suspicious eyes probed my face.

'Man U,' I admitted. They say confession's good for your soul, but it's bad for your health.

For a moment or two there was a stunned silence.

Then a loud exclamation. 'Flaming hell!'

Next thing I knew there was a jarring shock to the base of my skull. My bag flew one way and my brain went the other. And that's how I got my nickname, the Slap-on-the-head Kid.

Doherty never missed a chance after that. A trip in the corridor, a sly thump in games, a punch on the way out of the gates. He and his mates were the hounds and I was the hare. A few of the other kids looked sympathetic, but they didn't do anything. More than their faces were worth. After all, I *was* a Manc and you know what there is between Manchester and Liverpool? That's right. Needle.

'Them lads been after you again?' Mum asked one night when I got home.

'Yes.'

'Five on to one?'

'Yes.'

'Right, I'm going down to that school tomorrow.'

I nearly died. 'No, Mum. Please.'

'Well, we've got to do something,' she said.

'No way,' I said. 'You'll make things worse. They'll say I'm a grass.'

And that's when my nan came up with the idea. 'Karate,' she said. 'Or boxing. Something to toughen the lad up. Show he won't be pushed around.'

So the next Wednesday night I'm down at the Carmel Boxing Club, my stomach turning over at the sight of the ring and the bags. Me, the Slap-on-the-Head Kid, *boxing*. Who was I kidding? I was about as hard as reinforced blancmange. I was starting to think I was going to end up the Punch-in-the-Face Kid too! Only I'd been kicked around so long down at Stanley Comp. I was up for it. Anything was better than being a human doormat.

'When do I get to fight?' I asked, looking round the gym. Everybody laughed.

'Who are you laughing at?' I demanded hotly, which made them laugh even louder.

'Listen, son,' said the main man, walking towards me. 'First things first. What's your name?' I told him.

'I'm Tommy McAteer. Call me Tommy Mac.'

I didn't call him anything. I'd noticed this huge poster on the wall. 'You can run,' it said. 'But you can't hide.'

It made me think of Chris Doherty, and the smell of fear, and every time I'd had my face shoved into the lockers. Right, Tommy Mac, I thought, teach me to fight.

Except he didn't. He taught me press-ups and tuck jumps, sit-ups and stride jumps, snake presses and split jumps, V sit-ups and pike jumps, dorsal raises and star jumps. But no fighting.

I glanced at the other boys, a dozen or so aged from eleven to fifteen. When do I get to fight, I wondered, and which one of you will it be? But there was no fighting. We did bags and shadow boxing, pads and skipping. But still no fighting.

'Right, boys,' said Tommy Mac. 'Show me Mickey Mouse.'

I couldn't believe it. There's all these really tough-looking kids, holding their thumbs to their temples, palms facing out like big rodent ears.

'On guard,' said Tommy Mac. 'Fists.'

And the kids closed the Mickey Mouse ears into fists. So that's what it was for, to get your hands right in these bright red eight-ounce gloves.

'Tight fists,' said Tommy Mac. 'Tuck those arms in. Now, fighting mode. Elbows in.'

The next thing I knew he was poking at my arms. Like I was an oven-ready chicken or something.

'I said elbows in. Where are you from, Terry?'

'M–m–m . . .'

'You what?'

'Manchester.'

'Right, Manchester,' said Tommy Mac without blinking an eyelid. 'Use your feet to move around.'

I tried, but my feet didn't seem keen on the idea.

'Feet, feet, feet,' roared Tommy Mac, while the other kids laughed. 'If you've forgotten, they're the things on the end of your legs.'

'I haven't forgotten,' I said. 'But when do I get to fight?'

Tommy Mac just smiled. I didn't fight then either. Not that week, not the next. It was like a PE lesson, only harder. And still I was getting shoved around by Doherty and Co.

This, I told myself, is pathetic.

It wasn't though. Pathetic, I mean. I was enjoying it. It was the same routine each time. Light running to warm up. Tuition. On guard. Drills. Foot movements and stuff. Then bags, skipping, pads, some shadow boxing. But no fighting.

'Listen, Tom,' I said eventually. 'What is this, boxing or ballet?'

Tommy Mac didn't answer. He just gave me the eye the way he always did. A wry, wrinkly examination that told me I'd said something stupid.

'Gather round, boys,' he said. 'Terry wants a scrap. Tell him. Punch or defence – which is the most important?'

'Defence,' they chorused.

'Right,' said Tommy Mac approvingly. 'Anybody can punch. A kangaroo can punch. It's stopping a punch that matters.' He nodded to one of the older lads. 'Get a left-handed glove on, Terry. In the ring with the big feller.'

Was this it? Would I be fighting at last?

'Okay, Terry. Somebody throws a jab, concentrate on the jab. Jab him in the face.'

I jabbed at my opponent, but he smacked my fist away with his forearms.

'See, he deflects you. He's blocking you. Now change round.'

I watched my opponent take up the on guard position.

'See this lad?' said Tommy Mac.

See him? I couldn't miss him. He was a monster.

'He's got a powerful back hand. But don't worry, there are numerous ways to stop it. You can block it before it comes out. You've got to deflect it, or get out of the way. You can stop it if you get the block on early. Now block, block, block.'

The big feller's first shots stung, then slowly the punches lost their force.

'Now,' said Tommy Mac, 'There's nothing left in it. It's a baby punch.'

From then on I never had any doubts. I'd seen a monster turned into a mouse. At least, I'd *felt* it. I still didn't fight, but I knew what Tommy Mac was doing. All the strength and the hurt that was Chris Doherty had been a mystery before. Suddenly I knew where it was coming from. And I knew how to block it.

One evening I arrived early. There was only me and Tommy Mac in the gym.

'Sit down, lad,' he said. 'So who is it you're so keen to fight anyway?'

I told him.

'It's not my game,' said Tommy Mac. 'I'll teach you to box, not to be a street-fighter.'

'It's my fight, Tom,' I answered.

'That's right, son. It is.'

And that was it. Not another word about Doherty. Not a mention of the bad blood between us. The needle. But somehow when Tommy Mac started the session that evening I had the oddest feeling he was talking directly to me.

'Come on, you lazy rats,' he barked, halfway through the star jumps. 'If you give up in your exercises, you'll give up on anything. Be a winner, *win*.'

That was it. Be a winner. Win.

Next day I was shoving my PE bag in my locker when along came Doherty. His elbow caught my head and I pitched forward into the locker door.

'Aw,' he said sarcastically. 'I'm awful sorry. Did it hurt?'

'Not half as much as this would,' I yelled, and I drove my fist into the lockers. Every bit of strength coming right up from the floor and stabbing through my straight arm. You should have heard the way the lockers rattled and crashed.

Doherty's face sagged, but he wasn't ready to back off yet. 'You're mental,' he said. 'Yeah, a mental Manc.'

That was it. I hit him in the chest and watched with satisfaction as he staggered back against the wall. Only I'd forgotten his mates. Doherty had got his. Now I had mine. Four on to one. Punching, kicking, stamping. And me, I was trying to focus – bobbing, weaving, deflecting, blocking. Boxing. I lost, of course. Tommy Mac was good, but he wasn't about to turn me into Mike Tyson overnight. By the time one of the kids had run for a teacher I'd been well battered.

'Who did this?' the teacher demanded.

I could see Doherty looking at me.

'Some fourth year,' I murmured. 'He legged it.'

'Some fourth year,' Doherty repeated as the teacher walked away. 'Nice one. Just stick to that story and you'll do.'

At the time I felt really stupid. I'd fought and I'd lost. Now it was only going to get worse. It didn't though. Weeks passed before I realized how important two words can be.

'*You'll do.*'

That had been Doherty's way of signing the truce. And it's never been broken. He's still a moron, of course. But a moron who steers clear, and that suits me just fine. Anyway, like I said, it's my first show tonight. I'm up against this Connolly kid from Everton. I hear Tommy Mac beside me as I get in the ring.

'All set, Terry?'

'Yes.'

'Nervous?'

'Yes.'

'You wouldn't be human if you weren't. Don't forget, son. Never give up. Be a winner.'

I smiled. No sweat, Tommy Mac, I already am.

Mayday!*
Redvers Brandling

Captain Ian Sercombe was frightened. He rested a broad forefinger on the control column of the Boeing 747 and eased back in his seat. Glancing out of the cabin windows at the sixty metres of his giant machine's wingspan, he tried to calm himself with thoughts of its size and detail . . . as high as a six-storey building, over two hundred kilometres of wiring, four million parts, space for more than four hundred passengers . . .

'Decent night, Skip.'

First Officer Les Bright's voice cut in on Ian's thoughts. The two men had completed the pre-take-off check and were sitting on the flight deck. Outside a huge moon hung in the hot tropical night sky which pressed down on Singapore's Changi Airport.

Les Bright was talking to the control tower when Cabin Service Director Edwina Reeves came into the flight deck area.

'Two hundred and sixty passengers and thirteen cabin crew all safely on board, Captain. Cabin secure.'

'Thanks, Edwina,' replied Ian. 'We should be off very soon.'

Minutes later, the huge aircraft began to roll away from its stand at the airport. The time was 8.04 p.m. and the journey to Perth, Australia, had begun.

Within an hour all was routine on the flight deck. The Jumbo was cruising at Flight Level 370, about seven miles above sea level. Speed was 510 knots and the course was

*This story is based on a real-life incident

160° magnetic as the plane, under the automatic pilot, headed south over Indonesia.

'Weather ahead looks good,' commented First Officer Bright, nodding at the weather radar screen which promised three hundred miles of smooth flying ahead.

'Hmmm,' agreed Ian.

He had been studying the weather radar with unusual intensity – just as he had all the other complex instruments in the cabin. But the fear wouldn't go away. It wasn't nervousness . . . or apprehension . . . Ian Sercombe was frightened. He could only ever remember feeling like this once before, and that had been the dreadful day of the accident . . . .

Ian and his lifelong friend Mike Payne had been crewing together on a flight back from New York. Leaving the airport in Ian's car, they were accelerating on the M25 when a tyre burst. In the crash which followed Ian had been unhurt, but Mike was killed instantly. Just before the tyre went Ian had felt this unreasoning fear. Afterwards he could never quite rid himself of guilt for Mike's death. He'd been blameless perhaps – he'd checked the tyres just a couple of days previously – but how could Mike know that? Once again he thought of Mike's bluff, smiling Irish face, grinning as always and clapping those gloved hands together. Always been a joke between them that – the only pilot who never flew without wearing fine kid gloves.

Ian's thoughts were brought back to the present as First Officer Bright made a routine position report.

'Jakarta Control, Moonlight Seven over Halim at 20.44.'

Then it started.

'Unusual activity on weather radar, Captain.'

'I see it, Les.'

'Just come up – doesn't look good.'

'Could be some turbulence in that. Switch on the "Fasten Seat Belts" sign.'

The two pilots tightened their own seat belts. Behind them in the crowded cabins, passengers grumbled as they had to interrupt their evening meal to fasten their seat belts. Smiling stewardesses assured them there was no problem.

'Engine failure – Four!'

The flight engineer's terse voice cut the flight deck silence.

'Fire action Four,' responded Ian simultaneously.

Together Les Bright and Engineer Officer Mary Chalmers shut off the fuel lever to Four and pulled the fire handle. There was no fire in the engine and Ian felt an easing of his tension.

No pilot likes an engine failure, but the giant Jumbo could manage well enough on the three that were left.

'Engine failure – Two.'

Mary Chalmers' voice was more urgent this time, but as she and Les Bright moved to another emergency procedure she suddenly gasped breathlessly.

'One's gone . . . and Three!'

Seven miles high with two hundred and seventy-three people on board, the Boeing was now without power. Ian knew that the huge plane could only glide – and downwards.

'Mayday, Mayday, Mayday!' First Officer Bright's voice barked into the emergency radio frequency. 'Moonlight Seven calling. Complete failure on all engines. Now descending through Flight Level 360.'

Ian's hands and mind were now working with automatic speed. He again checked the fuel and electrical systems. Emergency restarting procedures failed to have any effect. Quickly he calculated their terrible position. The plane was dropping at about two hundred feet per minute . . . which meant that in twenty-three minutes' time . . .

'You two,' said Ian quietly to the First Officer and Flight Engineer. 'I'm going to need all the help I can get later on, but there could be problems back there with the passengers now – especially as we're obviously going down. Go back – help out – and get back here as soon as you can.'

Bright and Mary Chalmers climbed out of their seats, slamming the door to the flight deck behind them as they went to try and reassure the terrified passengers.

Ian was now alone on the flight deck.

'Problems,' he muttered aloud. 'Crash landing in the sea so keep the wheels up, lights are going to fail because there's no generated power from the engines, standby power from the batteries won't last long . . .'

The closing of the flight deck door interrupted Ian's monologue.

'All right back there?' he asked, as the First Officer climbed back into his seat. He was just able to make out his fellow pilot's quick nod in the rapidly dimming light on the flight deck.

'It's too risky to try and get over those mountains now,' said Ian. 'What do you think?'

'Go for the sea,' was the reply, in a strangely muffled tone.

Ian's arms were aching from holding the lurching and buffeting aircraft, but he was surprised when the First Officer leaned over and laid a hand on his shoulder. It seemed to have both a calming and strengthening effect.

'I'll take her for a while.'

The giant plane continued to drop. At 14,000 feet the emergency oxygen masks had dropped from the roof for passengers' use. Now the rapidly dropping height was down to 13,000 feet.

'I'll save myself for the landing,' muttered Ian, watching his co-pilot in admiration. In the dim light the First Officer was a relaxed figure, almost caressing the jerking control column. His touch seemed to have calmed the aircraft too. Its descent seemed smoother, almost gentle even.

13,000.

12,000.

11,000.

'Ian.'

The captain was startled by the unexpected use of his Christian name by the First Officer.

'Volcanic dust and jet engines don't mix. I think we should make another re-light attempt on the engines now.'

Still feeling calm, even relaxed considering the terrible situation they were in, Ian began the engine restarting drill yet again.

'Switch on igniters . . . open fuel valves . . .'

As suddenly as it had failed, Engine Four sprang back into life.

'We've got a chance!' cried Ian.

'Go for the rest,' was the quiet reply.

Expertly, Ian's hands repeated the procedure. There was a lengthy pause then . . . Bingo! Number Three fired . . . then One . . . and then Two.

'We'll make it after all,' sighed Ian, once again taking a firm grip of the controls.

'Les – get on to Jakarta Control and tell them what's happening . . . Les . . .'

To his astonishment, when Ian looked to his right only the gently swaying control column came into view. The First Officer had gone. It was then that the captain heard the crash of the axe breaking through the door to the flight deck.

Engineer Chalmers was the first one through the shattered door.

'Fantastic, Skipper, fantastic – how did you do it?'

'Incredible!'

This was Les Bright's voice.

'The flight deck door jammed and we've been stuck out there for five minutes wondering how on earth you were getting on – and now this! You're a marvel, Skipper.'

Ian glanced up at the animated face of his First Officer in the brightening light of the flight deck.

'But . . .'

The rest of the words died on his lips. A feeling of inexplicable gratitude and calm swept over him. He remembered the confident, sure figure who had so recently sat in the co-pilot's seat. Now he remembered too that just before the lights had reached their dimmest he had noticed that the hands holding the controls were wearing a pair of fine kid gloves.

'Get on to Jakarta,' Ian said quietly. 'Tell them we're coming in.'

Worms
John Gatehouse

1

Jeremy loved worms.

He loved to hold their juicy, fat, slimy bodies in the palm of his hand.

Sometimes he would twine one around his index fingers and then slowly pull in opposite directions until its body ripped in two.

'Uggh! That's gross!' screamed his sister, Annabel, when Jeremy showed her his latest trick. 'You really are weird, Jeremy.'

Jeremy didn't care what his sister thought. Or anyone else for that matter.

In his bedroom, he kept a large glass tank which was filled with his collection of worms. He would watch for hours as they tunnelled through the earth of his worm-farm.

And, when they grew large enough, he would take them out of the tank and put them in his lunchbox and sneak them into school.

Jeremy's favourite trick was to wait until the class was quiet and everyone was working. Then he would take a worm out of his lunchbox and drop it down the neck of a girl in front of him. Their shrieks and screams made the boring school day more fun than a trip to the circus.

Of course, Jeremy's tricks made sure he was always in trouble with his teachers, but this didn't worry him.

Jeremy didn't like people. He liked worms.

But the worms didn't like Jeremy.

2

'I bet you wouldn't!' said Andrew, sneering.

'I bet I would!' said Jeremy.

He was standing in the school playing field, surrounded by a group of boys from his class. Between his fingers he held a big, fat worm.

'All right,' said Andrew, holding up a bag of sweets. 'I bet you all these gobstoppers that you won't eat that worm.'

Jeremy smiled. A hush had fallen over the group. Everyone was staring at him, daring him on.

He knew what they were thinking: *He won't do it!*

But Jeremy would.

And he did.

He put one end of the worm between his fat lips and sucked.

'Yuck! That's disgusting!' cried Kamal, as the other end of the worm disappeared into Jeremy's mouth.

The boys ran off, laughing, to tell their friends.

Andrew threw the bag of sweets to Jeremy, before running after them. 'You win, Jeremy. But Kamal's right. That is disgusting!'

Jeremy waited until the boys were out of sight.

Then he quickly spat out the worm he had been hiding under his tongue. He felt sick.

'Ucck! That'll teach them not to believe me!' he said, speaking to the worm that now lay wriggling about on the wet grass. 'But I'll never do that again. You taste revolting!'

And, just because he wanted to, he stamped his foot hard on the worm before running off to wash out his mouth.

On the ground, dozens of worms burrowed up to the surface of the field.

They all lifted their heads in the direction Jeremy had taken.

3

If there was one teacher Jeremy hated it was Mrs Corbalt, who taught history. So that afternoon, when she had left the class to fetch some books, Jeremy took his chance.

He pulled the lunchbox from his holdall, and quickly walked up to the front of the class.

The other children knew that Jeremy was up to something.

'What are you doing, Jeremy?' whispered Leanne nervously.

Jeremy growled. 'Bug off!'

He pulled up the lid of Mrs Corbalt's desk and emptied out the contents of the lunchbox.

The classroom door opened.

'Jeremy, what are you doing?' demanded Mrs Corbalt, entering the room.

Jeremy smiled sweetly. 'Just wanted a new pencil, miss,' he lied, shutting the desk lid.

'Then ask me first!' Mrs Corbalt snapped, pushing Jeremy aside.

She opened her desk and let out a terrifying scream.

Wriggling all over her files and chalk were dozens of dirty, slimy worms.

Of course, Jeremy was sent to the headmaster.

'I'm sending a note home to your parents,' Mr Hunter told him. 'And you will not be going to the ice rink with the rest of your class on Friday.'

Jeremy didn't care. He didn't like ice skating. He always fell over and the other kids laughed at him and called him a beached whale.

When school ended, Jeremy walked home across the playing fields by himself. He was glad he had scared Mrs Corbalt. It had brightened up the day.

One by one, the worms crawled through the grass, following him.

4

That night, Jeremy dreamt that he had turned into a worm.

Not a small, common-or-garden worm, but a great big fat slug of a worm, the size of Jeremy himself.

This didn't surprise him. He had read a lot of books about worms and knew that some worms in Australia could reach the size of three metres. Compared to them, he was tiny.

He couldn't tell which end was his head and which end was his feet, not that he had feet any more because he was a worm.

Jeremy wasn't sure he liked being a worm.

For a start, he felt hungry, but worms, as far as he knew, didn't eat the food Jeremy liked to eat. No more burgers-and-chips for Jeremy the Worm.

Instead, he found himself burrowing down into the earth, feeding on the soil.

I'm eating mud! cried Jeremy to himself, not liking it one bit.

Suddenly, the ground shook, and he felt himself being lifted up into the sunlight.

He crashed onto the grass, wriggling madly about, trying to escape.

Looking up, he could see a giant-sized human child standing over him, holding a spade.

The child smiled. The sort of smile Jeremy smiled before he pulled a worm in two.

The child lifted up the spade and brought the blade crashing down towards Jeremy the Worm's big, fat body.

*

Jeremy woke up with a scream.

It was only a nightmare! he told himself, before pulling back his covers to cool down.

He looked down at his sheets.

They were covered in mud.

5

Jeremy was in a bad mood the following morning.

He was always in a bad mood, but not as bad as today. After his dream, he had been too scared to go back to sleep.

It was the mud on his sheets that had upset him. *Where had it come from?*

'I must have got mud on my feet when I was walking across the playing fields yesterday,' he told himself. But he couldn't remember seeing mud on his shoes.

He stared at the worms in his worm-farm. They were pressed against the glass, almost as if they were looking at him.

'Leave me alone!' he screamed, and ran out of the room.

When Jeremy was in a bad mood, he liked to take it out on anyone within reach. So he poured a glass of fruit juice over the picture Annabel was drawing on the breakfast table.

'Serves you right!' he said, when she started crying. 'You shouldn't have got in my way.'

He decided to leave his worms at home today. He didn't fancy the thought of carrying them around with him.

At school, Jeremy sat quietly in class. He didn't feel like bullying anyone.

'Jeremy! Stop daydreaming!' said his teacher sternly. 'Get your books out and get on with your work.'

Muttering rude words to himself, Jeremy reached into his holdall and grabbed hold of something squishy in his hand. Quickly pulling it back out, as if he had been burnt, he found himself holding a handful of big, fat worms . . .

6

Jeremy's screams made all the children jump in fright.

'Jeremy! What's the matter?' demanded Mr Harcourt.

Jeremy couldn't speak. He kept looking at the worms he had dropped on the floor. They were wriggling all over his shoes.

The other children started giggling.

Mr Harcourt scooped up the worms in his hand and threw them out of the window.

'What were you going to do with those worms, Jeremy?' he demanded. 'Put them in my desk to frighten me?' Mr Harcourt had heard all about Jeremy's tricks.

'No, sir,' whispered Jeremy.

'I don't believe you,' said his teacher angrily. 'And if I catch you with any more worms in this school, I'll put you on suspension. Now sit down!'

Jeremy sat, and he brooded. He knew how those worms had got into his bag. It was rotten Annabel. She must have put them there to pay him back for ruining her soppy picture.

Well, he'd get his revenge.

Jeremy was glad when the dinner bell sounded. He was still in a foul mood, so he pushed himself to the head of the queue. Anyone who complained was given a punch on the arm.

'Potatoes, bacon and spaghetti,' said Mrs Martin, the school dinner lady, as she passed Jeremy a plate of food.

Pushing past the other children, Jeremy sat down at the table. He was starving!

He lifted off the lid and looked down at his plate.

Next to the bacon slices and potatoes were dozens of small, thin, wiggling worms.

7

Jeremy jumped up, knocking over the dinner table. It crashed to the ground. Everyone in the dining hall turned their heads to look at him.

Mr Harcourt was in the hall, making sure the children didn't become too boisterous. He hurried over to Jeremy who stood staring at the floor, shaking.

When the teacher saw the worms on the floor next to Jeremy's dinner, he grabbed hold of the boy and frog-marched him out of the hall.

'Hey, leggo!' cried Jeremy, after he had been pushed along to the headmaster's office. 'I haven't done anything. It was the worms!'

'Don't be stupid,' shouted Mr Harcourt. 'How could those worms have got onto your plate unless you put them there? It was just another silly trick to scare the other children!'

Mr Harcourt told the headmaster all that had happened. Jeremy didn't stand a chance.

'I'm suspending you for a week,' said Mr Hunter, who was just as angry as Mr Harcourt. 'Collect your belongings and go straight home. And I'll be phoning your mother to let her know why you're not in school.'

Jeremy walked home, furious. If his sister had put those worms in his bag, then who put some on his dinner plate? It was hardly likely to have been Mrs Martin.

Turning into the park, Jeremy looked closely around at the flower beds. He pushed his hand in the earth, and pulled out worm after worm.

Throwing the worms on the ground, he stamped his foot down hard upon them.

'I HATE YOU! I HATE YOU!' he screamed.

8

Jeremy's mother was waiting for him when he got home.

'Your headmaster has just phoned me,' she said, looking as angry as Jeremy had ever seen her. 'I don't know why you played those stupid tricks, but you won't get away with it!'

Jeremy pretended to listen while his mother scolded him, ordering him to get rid of the worms, but his mind was on other things. Like how to pay his sister back for getting him into trouble.

And what he was going to do with his worms.

When Annabel arrived home, she seemed to know that she was in Jeremy's bad books. Instead of going out to play in the garden, the way she usually did, she kept close to her mother so that Jeremy couldn't thump her.

Frustrated, Jeremy stormed upstairs and slammed the door. He stared darkly at the worms in the worm-farm. They seemed to be laughing at him.

Jeremy snatched up the glass tank and carried it to his opened window.

'Get lost!' he screamed, and emptied the earth and worms onto the grass below.

He sat on his bed, gasping for breath. Now that the worms were gone, he felt a lot happier.

And since his rotten mother had grounded him for a whole fortnight, he decided to have an early night.

Outside, as the evening grew darker, hundreds of worms crawled through the wet grass towards his bedroom window.

9

Jeremy was asleep.

He knew that because he was having another dream about the worms.

This time, he lay in his bed, unable to move, as hundreds of worms crawled all over his body.

They moved across his legs and arms, slipping and sliding, and across his face and through his hair. Jeremy wanted to scream, but he was too scared to open his mouth in case a big fat worm crawled inside.

The worms wriggled across his stomach, and over his shoulders, wet and slimy, their bodies moving back and forth like a caterpillar's.

Wake up! Jeremy told himself. *It's not real!!*

He struggled to open his eyes. They felt heavy with sleep. When he did open them, he let out a gasp of relief.

There were no worms on him. He couldn't see a rotten worm anywhere in the room. It had only been a dream, and a horrible one, at that. But Jeremy didn't have to be afraid. He had got rid of his worms. They couldn't hurt him any more.

Under the covers, something moved across Jeremy's feet.

Startled, he wrenched the covers onto the floor and looked down at the end of the bed.

The white sheet was lost beneath a pool of dirt-stained, wriggling brown bodies.

The worms had come home to Jeremy.

10

The worms slithered across Jeremy's legs. They raised their heads as one, looking up at him.

Jeremy screamed and rolled out of bed. His head struck the bedside table as he landed with a thump onto the floor.

Leaping to his feet, and ignoring the pain in his head, he screamed again and again, slapping his legs with his hands in case there were any worms left on him. His mother, father and sister burst into the room, looking worried.

'Jeremy? What's the matter?' demanded his father.

Then he saw the worms crawling all over the bed.

'Jeremy, I've told you before to get rid of those horrible creatures!' shouted his mother. 'Look at the mess you've made! And why aren't they in their tank?'

Jeremy tried to explain, but no one believed him. His mother told him that he would be going to the doctor, the very next day. He needed something for his nerves, she said.

Jeremy watched numbly while his father collected up all the worms in a shoebox and took them outside. He was shaking. He started to cry.

I never want to see another worm in my life, he thought.

In the garden, under the light of a full moon, the worms tunnelled their way deep down back into the earth.

There they would stay, waiting.

Waiting for another boy like Jeremy.

The author would like to point out that no worm was injured during the writing of this book.

Cocky and Clive
Robert Swindells

I want to tell you about the two best friends I ever had.

It all happened in the summer of 1940, when I was ten. World War Two was on, and my dad had been killed the previous winter serving with the Navy. Mum said I must always remember that my dad had been a hero, and I *knew* he had, and that was the trouble.

You see, I *wasn't* a hero. There was this lad at school, Clive Simcox. He was the same age as me – in fact we were in the same class – but Clive was taller and heavier, and for some reason that summer he started picking on me. I didn't like fighting, so I tried to please him by letting him win at marbles and stuff like that, but it didn't work. He'd take my marbles, then ambush me on the way home from school and bash me up. He'd lie in wait in the mornings too, and trip me as I ran past. I'd arrive at school with grazed knees and dirt on my blazer and red eyes from crying, and everybody would know Clive had had another go at me.

I used to think, if I was a hero like Dad I'd face up to Simcox and punch him on the nose, even if he beat me up after. Sometimes, lying in bed in the morning, I'd convince myself that *this* time I was going to do it. This time I'd turn with my fists up and give him the biggest surprise of his life, but I never did. When it came to it – when he was actually there in front of me with his red face and mocking eyes – I'd either try to run or let him hit me to get it over with. I was ashamed of myself but I couldn't help it.

One hot afternoon when I got in from school, I found Mum talking with a pilot in the garden. There was an aerodrome outside the village – a fighter unit – and I guessed he was stationed there. I'd managed to dodge Clive so I was fairly presentable. 'Jim,' smiled Mum, 'this is Pilot Officer Cochrane. He helped me home with my shopping.'

I was completely bowled over. Fighter pilots were legendary figures in 1940, and this one *really* looked the part. Tall he was, and slim, with black hair and a good tan. I'd never been close to one before, and when he stuck his hand out I stood gaping.

'Well, Jim?' laughed Mum. 'Aren't you going to shake hands?' 'Uh? Oh, yes.' I shoved my paw out and he gripped it, grinning like that film star with the funny name. Bonar somebody or other. He had strong white teeth and flashing eyes, and I wondered fleetingly what he'd think if he knew he was shaking hands with a coward.

'Name's Mike,' he said, 'but my friends call me Cocky. I hope *we're* going to be friends, Jim.'

I could hardly believe it. A fighter pilot for a friend! They'd be green with envy at school. I looked at him. 'Do you spy a Flitfire – I mean, fly a Spitfire?' He roared with laughter. Mum laughed too. I felt myself blushing. 'No,' he chuckled. 'I don't spy a Flitfire – I high a Flurricane.'

He stayed to tea. It was only sardines on toast but we had it in the garden and I wished it could last for ever. He was *really* nice, and not a bit conceited. I was sure if *I* had wings on my tunic I'd be very conceited.

I couldn't wait to tell my chums next morning. By a wizard stroke of luck, Simcox missed me again so I was able to shove all that beastliness to the back of my mind while I basked in Cocky's reflected glory.

I told the story of one of his exploits. He hadn't talked about his exploits at all so I had to make one up, but it was good. 'Once,' I told a spellbound circle which included Simcox, 'flying alone on a dawn patrol, Cocky spotted a formation of 109s. There were nine of them, but he didn't hesitate. Putting his Hurricane into a shallow dive, he got their leader in his sights and blasted him out of the sky with a burst from his eight Brownings.'

The kids gasped and I glowed, bragging about my friend. 'As the leader disintegrated,' I said, 'Cocky flew right through the formation and came up underneath them, firing at another 109. This one flipped onto its back, trailing smoke, and the pilot baled out. Then, levelling off, Cocky shot a third Nazi out of the sky before zooming into the clouds, escaping before the remaining six knew what was happening.'

'Wow!' they went, and 'Golly!' I was flavour of the month, though we didn't have that expression in those days. It cut no ice with Simcox though. He went on tormenting me and I went on letting him.

Cocky started spending most of his free time at our house. I know now that he must have been sweet on Mum, but I didn't realize at the time. I thought he came to see *me*. And we *did* become friends. He made a kite which we flew together, and we went fishing too. Mum came with us sometimes, and sometimes it was just him and me. I loved being with him. I was proud to be seen in his company, as any boy would have been. The only slightly disappointing thing was that I could never get him to talk about his flying. I'd ask him things and he'd change the subject. He didn't get stroppy about it – I don't mean that – but he obviously preferred not to talk about it. Until the day I spilled the beans about Simcox.

We were on Windy Hill, flying the kite. I'd been brooding about my fear of Simcox, and it was spoiling my afternoon. Mum wasn't with us that day, and as we were packing up to go home I decided to make a clean breast of it. 'Cocky,' I said, 'I wish I was fearless like you.' He was winding the kite-string round the bit of dowelling we used as a hand grip. He laughed, glancing up at me. It was a short laugh, and there was no humour in it.

'Fearless?' He finished winding and handed me the kite. 'I'm not fearless, Jim. I'm petrified. Permanently petrified.'

I shook my head. I assumed he was joking. He was one of those people who can joke with a perfectly straight face. 'Oh yeah?' I grinned. 'Whoever heard of a petrified fighter pilot?'

'Nobody's *heard*, Jim,' he said. 'Everybody thinks we're fearless because that's what the newspapers say, but it's not true.' He sat down on the grass, looking away towards the aerodrome. I put the kite down and sat next to him. After a minute he said, 'The papers *have* to say we're fearless to keep people's spirits up, but we're not. None of us.' He plucked a stalk of grass and chewed the end. He wasn't looking at me. 'Do you know what happens when a Hurricane catches fire, Jim?'

I shook my head. I'd seen planes come down in flames – we all had, but they were always a long way off. Cocky went on gazing towards the aerodrome. 'What happens,' he said quietly, 'is that the fuel burns. Gallons and gallons of fuel. The slipstream blows the flames into the cockpit like a blowtorch, right into the pilot's face. If he gets out at once he might escape with blistered hands and cheeks. If he doesn't – and it usually takes a while to undo the harness and get the canopy off – those flames'll have destroyed his face and maybe his eyes as well. If he gets out then – if the pain hasn't caused him to faint – he's going to walk around for the rest of his life looking like something out of a horror story, even if he's not blind. And of course they don't always burn. A man might die in the cockpit, riddled with machine gun bullets or blown in two by a cannon shell, or sit screaming while his crippled plane spins into the sea.' He flung the stem away. 'One of those things happens to *somebody* every time we scramble, Jim, and we sometimes scramble four, five, six times a day. And while we're sitting around waiting for the call, we're thinking about the things I've just mentioned – about chums who've bought it recently. Remembering how old George, who used to be so handsome, looked in hospital with his lips and nose and eyelids gone – knowing that sooner or later it'll be *our* turn.' He lay down and gazed into the sky. 'And that's not the worst of it, Jim. The nights are the worst, because no matter how tired you are – and *I've* never known such tiredness – it's almost impossible to sleep. Your thoughts won't let you sleep. Is it my turn tomorrow? Will I burn? Will this bed be empty twenty-four hours from now? And if you *do* drop off, from sheer exhaustion, there are the nightmares.' He turned his head to look at me. 'And you think we're fearless, Jim? You think *I'm* not afraid?' He snorted. 'I've *puked*, laddie – got up out of my bed and puked at the thought of ever flying again. I'll tell you this, Jim. If I could – if I *dared* – I'd get up right now and start running, and I wouldn't stop till I was somewhere they'd never find me, and that's true of *all* fighter pilots – every one of us.' He sat up, wrapped his arms round his bony shins and rested his forehead on his knees. 'Only the insane are fearless, Jim. The rest of us carry on because we're trapped.'

I suppose it made me feel better, knowing Cocky was afraid. Knowing I wasn't the only one. It certainly destroyed my illusions about the glamour of war in the air, and it did something else as well. It caused me to watch Cocky closely whenever he was with us, and it quickly became evident that he'd told me the truth. To those who didn't know, including Mum, he remained the dashing, daredevil character with the infectious grin – a big, gangly schoolboy for whom the war, or at least his bit of it, was nothing but a ripping adventure. But if you were watching, the signs were there. The way he perched on the very edge of his chair. That twitchy eyelid. The lower lip caught between the teeth and the expression of utter desolation when he thought nobody was looking. It made me even more fond of him. He'd confided in me – told me things he wouldn't tell anybody else in the world. We were best friends.

One afternoon just before the start of the summer holidays, I was helping Mum get the tea when there was a knock on the open door. We looked round and saw a pilot on the step. He didn't say anything. He just stood holding his cap in both hands, looking at Mum. Mum gazed back for a moment, then said in a quiet voice, 'It's Cocky, isn't it?' The pilot nodded, stepping into the kitchen. 'This morning,' he murmured, 'near Deal. I am most awfully sorry,' and Mum began to cry. I stared from one to the other till it sank in, then ran howling to my room.

I don't know if you've ever lost your best friend. I hope not. If you haven't, it's no use my trying to describe to you how I felt. You'd have to feel it for yourself. Anyway I was ill all night, and Mum kept me off school next day.

The day after that – it was a Friday, the last day before the hols – I was trailing along the lane when suddenly Clive Simcox sprang out in front of me and snatched my cap. I don't know to this day what came over me, but before I knew what I was doing I'd clenched my fist and smashed it into the middle of Clive's face. He must've been *really* startled because he neither struck back nor covered up, but stood there with his mouth open while blood ran from both nostrils into his mouth. I wanted to punch him again, to go on punching for all the times he'd bullied me, and for Dad, and for Cocky, but I couldn't. We stood looking at each other, and then he snorted and shook his head and flung himself at me and I found myself flat on my back with the bully kneeling on my chest. Blood from his nose was dripping onto my face, so I turned my head to one side. I knew what he'd do. His favourite trick when he had somebody down was to grab a double handful of his victim's hair, just above the ears, and bang his head on the ground again and again. Kenneth Smith in Standard Two had to have stitches after Simcox did that to him. I bucked and writhed but it was no use – I couldn't shake him off, so I screwed up my eyes and prepared for the worst.

I suppose if I gave you three guesses, you wouldn't guess what happened next. There I was with my eyes closed waiting for the torture to start, and suddenly Clive Simcox burst into tears. As I opened my eyes to look at him, he sort of slid off me onto the ground and lay curled on his side with his hands over his face, rocking himself and sobbing. I didn't know what to do. I sat up and looked at him and after a bit I said, 'What's up?'

'My dad,' he choked. 'He's dead.' Simcox senior worked in some sort of factory. How could he be dead? 'Dead?' I gasped. 'How?'

'Yesterday. After that raid on the aerodrome.' Some enemy planes had bombed the aerodrome the day before. It was always happening but I still didn't understand. 'But – your dad's in a factory. What was he doing on the aerodrome?'

'He wasn't *on* the aerodrome,' he sobbed. 'A stick of bombs fell short. One hit a house near the factory. The house collapsed. Most of the people got out but a little girl was trapped. It was Dad's break. He crawled into the wreckage to get the kid, and the whole lot fell in on him.'

I understood then all right, but I still didn't know what to do so I laid a hand on his shoulder and said, 'He was a hero, your dad.' I thought it might help but it did the

opposite. A fresh howl burst from him and he cried, 'I know, and I was *ashamed* of him because he wasn't in the Army like everybody else's dad. I haven't even *talked* to him for months, and now it's too late.'

Well, most families had somebody to mourn in those days. People tried to help, meant to be kind, but in the end you just had to get through it. And you did get through it, but it changed you. It changed Clive Simcox all right. The bullying stopped. He'd been acting tough to make up for his dad not being in the Army, see? He thought kids were sneering behind his back and maybe they were, some of them. Anyway they gave Simcox senior a medal, and quite right too, and Clive had to go and be presented. That bucked him up a bit but it couldn't cancel out the thing that haunted him. Fifty years have gone by since then and he *still* wishes he'd been nicer to his dad. He doesn't go on about it but *I* know because we're best friends. You know – like Britain and Germany. Makes you wonder why we had to fight in the first place, doesn't it?

Chicken
Mary Hoffman

It was hard to say when the group became a gang. Perhaps it was when Mark Mason tried to hang around with us and we froze him out. Or perhaps when we started calling ourselves The Inliners. Definitely we were a gang by the time of the leadership struggle or there wouldn't have been a struggle to start with. And we'd never have been so stupid as to do the dares.

We had all known each other since Nursery. Alfie and I had hung out together since before we were born actually, because our mums were best friends and they'd gone into the hospital to have us on the same day.

Dylan, Jamal and Leon all live within a couple of streets of Alfie and me. (I'm Rick, by the way.) We all learnt to swim together in the local kiddie pool, all went to birthday parties at each other's houses dressed as Power Rangers or Ninja turtles, all went up to the Juniors at the same time, all played football on the common, all went to Woodcraft and went camping together, all got our first inline skates the same Christmas.

So had a lot of other kids, of course, but our group had been special from the beginning, enjoying in-jokes and making up a sort of private language that kept our other friends at a slight distance. We were all among the oldest and biggest in our year, because we had birthdays close to one another in September. Maybe that made us look more like a gang, like hard men. But there was nothing about us to worry our parents or our teachers – until we got into Year 6.

For the first time in our lives we were facing being split up. Alfie's parents were thinking of moving and Dylan's were putting him in for the Grammar School. Only me, Jamal and Leon were sure of being in the same secondary school and it made the whole group edgy. Maybe that's when we became a gang.

It was late October when the dares started. I suppose it was my fault really. We were just mucking about when I dared Alfie to steal some fireworks from Patel's. That's when Alfie should have said no and the whole thing would have stopped before it started. Then maybe *it* would never have happened. But he didn't.

It was pathetically easy. Mr Patel is a nice trusting man whose daughter Sushila is in our class. Alfie managed to smuggle two Skyburst rockets out under his blazer while the rest of us chatted to Mr Patel about the local football team.

Later, when we set the rockets off on the common, everyone was a bit hyper. Maybe that's when the rivalry between Alfie and Dylan started. Alfie was capering round like a mad thing, the bright explosion of coloured light from the rocket dyeing his face green and purple.

'One Alfie Spencer, there's only one Alfie Spencer,' he was chanting.

'Knock it off!' grunted Dylan. 'It was only a bit of shoplifting.'

'Yeah, well,' said Alfie. 'But look who didn't do it.'

'No one asked me to,' said Dylan indignantly. 'I would've done it if it was my dare.'

'Yeah,' said Alfie.

'Go on then,' said Dylan. 'Dare me and I'll show you.'

'Yeah, dare him, Alf,' said Jamal.

Alfie thought for a minute. Not shoplifting again; that was too easy.

'Okay, Dyl,' he said slowly. 'I dare you to get Old Knickers trick or treating.'

'Old Knickers' was Mrs Nixon, our headteacher. By common consent, her house was always avoided by trick or treat gangs at Hallowe'en. Mrs Nixon had strong views on what she called 'hooliganism'. And she made them very clear in assembly on November 1st.

'Much as I dislike that American import of tolerated blackmail called Trick or Treating,' she told the whole school assembly, 'I thought there were at least some rules to it. I thought children were supposed to ask which you'd prefer. Indeed I even had a bowl of fun-size chocolate bars ready by the door . . .'

Jamal and Leon turned to look at me. We had missed a trick there. Or rather a treat.

'But no one rang the bell,' continued Mrs Nixon, 'and this morning I discovered my car had been decorated with pink silly string and my garden hedge was festooned with loo paper.' She glared at us and Dylan stared straight ahead.

'Lame,' whispered Alfie out of the corner of his mouth.

And so it continued all term. There was the guy of Old Knickers that was burnt at the bonfire party. That was Jamal's dare. The kidnap of Cooper, who was the ginger cat belonging to our form teacher, Miss Jellicoe. That was Leon's, only he got caught, because he was covered in scratches. He wouldn't have hurt Cooper; Leon was soppy about all animals. He was supposed to send a ransom note for £20, but Cooper escaped and ran home.

Then there was the fire in a wastepaper basket, which set off the smoke alarms and called out the fire-brigade. That was mine, I'm now ashamed to say, and it earned me a lot of admiration in the gang.

But the main rivalry was still between Alfie and Dylan. It got worse by the end of term, when Dylan sat the exam for the Grammar School. It seemed as if Alfie was determined to take him down a peg or two.

The Inliners were beginning to split into two. I could feel it happening and I didn't like it. I always backed Alfie, of course, and Jamal tended to support Dylan. Leon was the most easy-going of all of us, and refused to take sides.

And now our parents were getting really concerned. Leon's had been horrified about the cat incident but he had managed to persuade them that it was just a practical joke gone wrong. The school had begun to suspect us because all the incidents were connected with our form and, being big and bad-looking, as I say, the suspicion naturally fell on us, even though we'd never done anything like this before.

Then Alfie twisted his ankle quite badly trying to abseil down the school wall. I have to admit that I was helping him, but I wasn't the one who dared him to do it. All the dares now seemed to be between him and Dylan and they were getting worse. Alfie's parents asked a lot of awkward questions about what we'd been up to after dark that made him hurt his ankle, but at least no one saw us.

Then Dylan got horribly drunk doing the dare about having one glass of everything in his parents' drinks cabinet. His sick note said he had a tummy upset, but that was putting it mildly. I overheard my mum telling Alfie's it was alcohol poisoning and Dylan had had to go to hospital.

I tried to get Alfie to stop then, because it was clearly becoming dangerous, but he said it was Dylan's turn to dare him to do something next and he couldn't stop it because Dylan would call him chicken. Dylan came back to school looking very white and shaky and I saw him give Alfie an evil look at break-time. It was hard to believe that they had ever been friends.

And yet we were still all in the gang. Inliners for ever! We were all skating along the High Street together when Dylan said to Alfie, 'I dare you to take on the Terminator.'

If we hadn't been going downhill, I would have stopped. The Terminator was a boy at the comprehensive, about fourteen years old and already built like Arnie. He was Mark Mason's older brother, Tony, but everyone called him the Terminator and he liked it. Actually I don't know that he ever really did anyone any damage, but he was well over six feet tall and made of solid muscle. No one had ever tried to bully Mark, let's put it that way. Alfie wouldn't stand a chance against him and Dylan knew it.

I sped up and came level with Alfie. He was looking almost as green as he had that night by the light of the stolen rockets.

'Are you mad?' I hissed. 'You're not really going to do it? You'll end up as dogmeat. I might as well call the ambulance now.'

'What's the matter, Alf?' taunted Dylan, whizzing past. 'Are you chicken?'

Alfie straightened his back and concentrated on weaving in and out of the shoppers. I could see he was going to do it.

He didn't let me in on the plan this time, so I couldn't even be around to help him when the massacre took place. I never knew what exactly happened, but a couple of days later there was a ring at my doorbell, and Alfie fell on the doormat. He looked terrible. He had a black eye, which was closing up fast, and a thick lip and blood all down his cheek.

'I did it, Rick,' he gasped, rolling over and clutching his stomach.

'I'll ring the hospital,' I said.

'No, don't,' whispered Alfie. 'Let me stay here. My parents'll kill me if they find out. Specially so soon after the ankle thing.'

'How do you think they're not going to find out, with you looking like that?' I demanded.

Fortunately the matter was taken out of our hands, because my mum came out and saw him. And that was that. She rang Alfie's mum and then drove him straight to Casualty. I was allowed to come too and Alfie's mum met us there. The grown-ups were white-faced and quiet in that way that's so much more scary than shouting.

Alfie refused to say who had done it. He had no broken bones, thank goodness, only bruising. But all hell was let loose just the same. Old Knickers had a field day in assembly, going on about bullying, and the whole gang was put on report – which was very unfair, seeing as we hadn't done anything to Alfie. Except for Dylan of course.

I honestly thought it would end there, as soon as Dylan saw Alfie's face. He looked a bit peculiar, as if he might throw up. And if Alfie had been prepared to give it up, it might have all stopped before the worst happened. But Alfie had just been given the pounding of his life and he wasn't about to let Dylan off the hook.

Nothing happened for a week and it was nearly the end of term. I was beginning to breathe more easily. Alfie was a bit more quiet than usual but that was understandable. Then one day at break he took me to one side and said, 'Saturday afternoon. Silbury cuttings.'

My blood ran cold. I've often seen that written down, but that's actually what it feels like. As if icy water is being pumped through your veins. Silbury cuttings used to be notorious in our neighbourhood. A few years ago, a kid was killed on the railway line at Silbury cuttings. It was a result of a game of 'chicken' with the trains. Ever since then, it has been the biggest no-go area around. The number of lectures we've had in assembly about it, with the police as well, and the number of times our parents have spoken to us about it in their most serious voices – well, I just can't tell you how it made me feel to hear Alfie even mention it.

'You're kidding, right?' I said, knowing he wasn't.

'Never more serious,' said Alfie. 'Are you in, or not?'

I didn't know what to say. My mind was racing. My only hope was that the security was now much tighter round Silbury cuttings than it had been when the kid got killed. I swear Alfie could read my mind, because he reached into his bag and took out a pair of wire-cutters he'd pinched from his dad's toolbox.

I decided to play along with Alfie, till I could work out what to do. I told him I was in, then as soon as I could, I got Jamal and Leon on their own.

'Silbury cuttings!' said Jamal. 'No way! That's going too far.'

Leon agreed and I was hugely relieved. Surely if all three of us said no, we could stop it? I mean, we didn't have votes or anything, but it was three against two, always assuming Dylan would even accept the dare. We should have known better.

We caught up with Alfie and Dylan before school on Friday. They were standing near the gate deep in conversation. I felt a pang; it was like the good old days when we were all just best mates. Until we got close to them and we could see the look in their eyes.

They just refused to listen. Dylan said Alfie had set us all up to put him off, because then he could call him chicken. He was particularly disgusted with Jamal. So I did the unforgivable: I told them I'd tell their parents.

Alfie and Dylan rounded on me with identical looks of fury.

'If you do,' hissed Alfie, 'it'll be the end of you and me.'

I thought about being friends since before we were born.

'And,' he added, 'it won't even stop us. We'll just do it another time, when they've forgotten about it. They can't watch us for ever.'

I felt absolutely paralysed. The best we could do was to say that we wouldn't be there and that we thought they were both mad. We walked away into the school building and that was the moment I knew the Inliners had ended for ever.

But, of course, I did go to Silbury cuttings on Saturday afternoon and so did the others. I think we couldn't bear not to know what was going on. We squeezed through the gap in the wire fencing that Alfie had made with his father's cutters. Then we slid down the embankment and hid behind some bushes. We could see them, Dylan and Alfie, standing by the railway line like a couple of trainspotters. My mouth was dry. I could hear a train coming.

It streamed past and I had no idea what had happened. It was all noise and speed and confusion. I realized my eyes were shut. When I opened them, I could have cried with relief. Alfie and Dylan were both still standing there. But they seemed to be arguing. I caught the words 'not ready' before the wind whipped them away and I realized it wasn't all over. Dylan was still going to do it. I saw him step onto the line.

I think I must have gone a little mad then. I went charging down the embankment yelling. I don't even know what I was saying or what I intended to do. Wrestle them both to the ground and sit on them till they came to their senses? I was no Terminator.

There was another train coming. I grabbed Alfie, gibbering and crying like an idiot. The train was getting nearer. Dylan just stood there, white and frozen. He wasn't going to make it.

'Dylan!' I screamed, but he didn't seem to hear me. I didn't dare grab him. I still feel bad about that. I still have nightmares about it. Dylan standing on the line like a statue, me rooted to the spot, unable to move as the train got closer.

It was Alfie who moved. I felt him wrench himself away from my grasp and hurl himself towards Dylan. And then the train rushed by. I couldn't see them, couldn't hear anything but the screaming of wheels on rails. The slipstream from the speeding train knocked me over and I was out of it.

I came round hearing the others crashing down the embankment. Jamal and Leon helped me up and we saw the other two across the other side of the line. They were lying on the ground with their arms wrapped round one another, and there was a lot of blood.

Suddenly, there were shouts behind me. Policemen came down the embankment, talking urgently into their radios. They must have called the ambulance because that came flashing and nee-nawing along soon afterwards. It turned out someone had seen the hole in the chainlink fence and dialled 999. The police must have called the station too, because no more trains came by while the paramedics carried Dylan and Alfie away on stretchers.

The local papers tried to turn Alfie into a hero. He told me that was the worst part, having everyone praise him for saving Dylan's life, when his life wouldn't have been in any danger in the first place if it hadn't been for Alfie. He feels nothing but guilt about what happened. After all, he was okay, physically, just very shocked and bruised. But Dylan, well, his foot was so badly hurt, they had to amputate it.

He can't skate so well with his artificial one, but he still does it. We all still see each other. Alfie's parents didn't move away after all, and Dylan didn't pass his Grammar School exam, so we all ended up at the comprehensive. The funny thing is, although we're all still friendly, it's Alfie and Dylan who are best friends now.

Me and Alfie aren't as close as we used to be. I thought at first it was because he felt he owed Dylan one, but once he told me that it was more as if they had gone through a bad illness together and survived. 'It was a kind of madness,' he said.

We are definitely not a gang any more. Just a group of friends, who've known each other since Nursery. We wouldn't dare be anything else.

Barney
Will Stanton

August 30th

We are alone on the island now, Barney and I. It was a bit sad to have to sack Taylor after all these years, but I had no choice. The childish pranks he played I could have forgiven, but when he actually tried to poison Barney out of pure wickedness, he was standing in the way of scientific progress. And that I cannot allow.

I can only believe his attempt to poison Barney was made while he was under the influence of alcohol, it was so clumsy. The poison container was overturned and a trail of powder led to Barney's dish. Taylor's defence was pathetic: he tried to deny it! Since there was no one else on the island, who, apart from him, could have done it?

September 2nd

I don't feel so bad about sacking Taylor now. I suppose this isolated life on the island must have become too much for him. That, and having to abandon the use of his precious guinea pigs. He insisted right to the end that they were better suited than Barney to my experiments. He was a hard worker but not very bright, poor Taylor.

Anyway, now that I am by myself with Barney, I have complete freedom to carry on my work without interruption. And now Taylor has gone, it's amazing how much happier Barney seems to be! I have given him the complete run of the place, and what fun it is to see how his newly awakened mental curiosity carries him about. After only two weeks of the glutamic acid treatments, he has become interested in my library, dragging the books from the shelves and going over them page by page. I am sure he knows that there is some knowledge to be got from them – if only he knew how!

September 8th

For the past two days, I have had to keep Barney under strict observation – and how he hates being confined! I am afraid that after my experiments are finished I shall have to do away with Barney altogether. Ridiculous as it may sound, there is always a slight risk that he may be able to pass on his intelligence to others of his kind. However small the chance might be, the risk is too great to ignore. Fortunately, there is in the basement a vault built with the idea of keeping vermin out. It will do equally well to keep Barney in – for as long as necessary.

September 9th

It seems that I spoke too soon. Barney escaped! This morning I let him out for a moment to frisk around before we began a new series of tests. After a quick look around the room, he returned to his cage, sprang up on the door handle, removed the key with his teeth, and before I could stop him he was out of the window! By the time I reached the yard, I saw that he had got on to the coping-stones around the top of the well. I arrived on the spot only in time to hear the key splash into the water far below.

I confess I am rather embarrassed by this. It is the only key. The door is locked. There are some valuable papers in separate compartments inside the vaults. Fortunately, although the well is over forty feet deep, there are only a few feet of water in the bottom, so getting the key back

will not be too much of a problem. But I must admit that Barney has won the first round!

September 10th

I have had a rather upsetting experience. Once again, in a minor clash with Barney, I have come off second best. On this occasion, I will admit that he acted like a hero and may even have saved my life.

In order to help myself to get down into the well, I knotted a length of three-quarter inch rope at one-foot intervals to make a simple ladder. I reached the bottom easily enough, but after only a few minutes of groping for the key, my torch batteries ran out and I returned to the surface. A few feet from the top, I heard excited squeaks from Barney, and when I reached ground level I noticed that the rope was almost completely severed. It seems that it had rubbed against the edge of the stonework and Barney, seeing the danger I was in, was doing his best to warn me.

I have now replaced the worn section of rope. I have put new batteries into my torch, and I am now ready for the final descent down the well. I have taken these few minutes off to give myself a breather and to bring my diary up to date. Perhaps I should make myself a sandwich, as I may be down there longer than seems likely at the moment.

September 11th

Poor Barney is dead an soon I shell be the same. He was a wonderfull ratt and life without him is knot worth livving. If anybody reeds this, please do not disturb anything on the island but leeve it like it is as a shryne to Barney, espechilly the old well. Do not look for my body as I will throwe myself into the see. You mite bring a couple of young ratts an leeve them as a living memorial to Barney. Females – no males. I sprayned my wrist is why this is written so bad. This is my laste will. Do what I say an don't come back or disturb anything after you bring the young ratts like I said. Just females.

Goodby

Virtually True
Paul Stewart

Sebastian Schultz. It isn't the kind of name you come across every day. But there it was, large and clear, at the top of the newspaper article in front of me.

The reader of the newspaper was a big woman with heavy shoes, black tights and a tartan skirt. I couldn't see her face, but I could hear her wheezy breath.

MIRACLE RECOVERY, the headline said. *Sebastian Schultz, a 14-year-old schoolboy from South London, awoke yesterday from a coma that doctors feared might last for ever*. After that, the words got too small to read.

Sebastian, I thought. Sebastian Schultz. It couldn't be the Sebastian Schultz I'd met. That wouldn't be possible. But seeing the same name in the paper was a helluva coincidence. I leant forward to read the rest of the article.

Six weeks ago, schoolboy Sebastian Schultz was badly injured in a motorway accident. His condition, on arrival at the General Hospital, was described as critical though stable. Despite doctors' hopes, however, the boy did not regain consciousness. His parents, June and Ted Schultz, were informed that their son was in a coma.

At a press conference this morning, Mr Schultz admitted, 'That was the news we had been dreading.'

'You always pray it won't happen to you,' his wife added. 'We knew that the doctors were doing all they could but in our hearts we knew we needed a miracle.'

Now that miracle has happened . . .

At that moment, the woman shifted round in her seat, and her hand moved down the page. I suddenly saw the photograph that went with the story, and gasped. Although the boy in the picture was younger than the Sebastian I'd met, there was no doubt. They were the same person.

'But how?' I muttered.

'A-hem!' I heard, and looked up. Two beady black eyes were glaring at me from above the paper.

'I'm sorry, I . . .'

But the woman was not listening. Turning the page noisily, she laid the newspaper down on her lap – so I wouldn't be able to see the back, I suppose – and went on reading.

It didn't matter, though. I'd already seen all I needed to see. Sebastian Schultz, the boy I'd got to know so well recently, had apparently been in a coma for all that time. I felt nervous and shivery. It didn't make any sense. It didn't make any sense at all.

I sat back in my seat, stared out of the train window and ran through the events in my head. The more I remembered, the crazier the situation seemed to be.

It all started a month ago. Dad and I had spent the entire Saturday afternoon at the Rigby Computer Fair.

Dad's nutty about computers. He's got a Pentium 150 Mhz processor, with 256mb of RAM, a 1.2Gb hard disk drive and 16-speed CD-ROM, complete with speakers, printer, modem and scanner. It can do anything. Paint, play music, create displays – even when my homework's rubbish, it *looks* fantastic. If I could just get it to make the bed and fold up my clothes it would be perfect.

Best of all are the games. *Tornado*, *Megabash*, *Scum City*, *Black Belt*, *Kyrene's Kastle* – I've played them all. With the screen so big, and the volume up loud, it almost feels as if you're inside the games, battling it out with the *Zorgs*, *Twisters*, *Grifters*, or whatever.

Of course, Dad was never satisfied. Technology was advancing every day, and he couldn't resist any of the new gadgets or gizmos that came on the market.

That was why we went into Rigby for the Computer Fair. After hours of looking at what was on offer, we came away with a virtual reality visor and glove, and a handful of the latest interactive psycho-drive games. They're terrific. Not only do the visor and glove change what you see, but better than that, you can control the action by what you're *thinking*. Well cool!

When we got them, I thought the games were all new. Now, I'm not so sure. In fact I remember now that one of them had some brown spots on the plastic cover which I scraped off with my finger nail.

Anyway, back at home, Dad set everything up. I plugged myself in, switched on and launched myself off into the first of the games. It was called *Wildwest*.

That's what I like about computers. The more futuristic they get, the better you can understand the past. I wasn't standing in the converted loft – the Powerbase, as Dad calls it – any more. I was really there, striding down the dusty track through the centre of town. There was a sheriff's badge pinned to my shirt.

As I burst in through the swing doors of the saloon, everyone went silent and loads of shifty pairs of eyes turned and glared at me. I strode over to the bar – nonchalantly. 'Sarsaparilla!' I said and a glass of fizzy red stuff came sliding along the bar towards me. As I took a sip, a piano began playing and the conversation started up again.

Suddenly, I heard a loud crash behind me. I spun round. There, silhouetted in the doorway, was Black-Eyed Jed, the fastest gun in the west. 'This town ain't big enough for the both of us, Sheriff Dawson,' he drawled, and fingered his guns lightly. 'Let's see what you're made of, boy,' he sneered. 'Outside. Just you and me.'

I can remember grinning. This was *really* cool!

'You'll be smiling on the other side of your face when I've finished with you, Sheriff,' said Black-Eyed Jed.

I finished my drink and slammed the glass down on the bar. Jed had already left the saloon. All eyes were on me once again as I walked calmly back across the room. A man's gotta do what a man's gotta do, I thought happily, and wondered what sort of score I was notching up.

All at once, something strange happened. Something really strange. Up until that point, the game had been pretty much as I expected. But when the *second* sheriff appeared through the back door, shouting and waving his arms about, I realized that the game was more complicated than I'd thought.

'Don't go out!' the second sheriff shouted.

'And who are you? This town ain't big enough for the two of *us*,' I quipped.

'I'm serious,' the sheriff cried, and I knew he meant it.

'Who *are* you?' I said again. He wasn't like the other characters in the saloon. For a start, he was younger – about my age – and although he looked like a computer image, he somehow didn't move like one.

'There's no time to explain,' he shouted. 'Just follow me.'

I did what I was told. I'm not sure why. We raced down a corridor, and through a door. The room was full of smoke and men playing cards. We ran past them, and out through another door. A woman screamed, and hid herself behind a full-length mirror. As we walked by, I stopped and waved at my reflection.

Clever, I thought.

'Come ON!' shouted the other sheriff.

We went on through another door, and another, and another – and ended up back in the saloon.

'NO!' screamed the second sheriff. Then he ran to the back of the saloon and dived through the window. By the time I had climbed out after him, he was already sitting on a horse. 'Jump up!' he cried.

He kicked the horse, and we sped off in a cloud of dust.

'Who are you?' I asked for a third time.

But the second sheriff still didn't answer. He'd seen the posse of men on horseback speeding after us. 'Keep your head down,' he said.

At that moment, the sound of a gunshot echoed round the air. The second sheriff groaned, and his body slumped back against me. Ahead of me, in bright neon lights across the sky came a message.

GAME OVER.

As I slipped off the visor, the empty desert disappeared and I found myself back in the Powerbase. I took off the glove and headphones. My head was still echoing with the sound of the firing gun. I glanced at the score on the screen. 21,095. Then I noticed something else.

While I'd been in the Wild West, the printer had come on. I picked up the piece of paper from the tray.

At the top was a picture of the second sheriff. This time, though, he was wearing jeans, sweatshirt and trainers. Printed over the bottom of the photograph was a name. *Sebastian Schultz – 23 January 1985 – ?* Below it, a message: I'M STUCK. PLEASE HELP TO RETRIEVE ME. TRY 'DRAGONQUEST'.

Of course, I wanted to go straight into the game he'd suggested, but it was already half an hour after lights-out, and I didn't want Mum to have some reason for keeping me off the computer. Sebastian and *Dragonquest* would have to wait.

The next morning, I was up and back on the computer before the milkman came. By the time his float jangled and clinked its way along our street, I'd already walked through the massive studded doors of the dragon's castle lair.

The aim of the game was simple. I had to rescue the fair Princess Aurora from the wicked dragon, and collect as much of the creature's treasure along the way as I could. I'd already got loads of stuff by the time I reached the princess, who'd been imprisoned at the top of a tall tower. She was a young woman with incredibly long golden plaits.

'My hero!' she squealed. 'Take me away from all this.' Behind me, I could hear the dragon roaring as it pounded up the stairs. 'Make haste, my brave knight,' the princess said urgently. 'Rescue me now.'

'Never mind her,' came a voice, and a second knight appeared from the wardrobe. 'It's *me* who needs rescuing!'

'Fie! Pish! And fooey!' the princess complained. 'I'm the damsel in distress here, not you!'

The dragon was getting closer.

'Sebastian?' I said.

The second knight nodded. 'Quick,' he said. 'While there's still time.' And with that, he did something which really wasn't very gallant, considering he was meant to be a knight. He pulled out a huge pair of scissors and chopped off the princess's two long plaits. Then he tied them together, fixed one end round the bedpost and threw the other end out of the window.

'NOW!' he screamed, as he leapt for the window and disappeared from view down the hair rope.

At that moment, the dragon – a huge great scaly slobbering beast – appeared at the doorway. I gasped, and leapt for the window after Sebastian. As I lowered myself down I felt the dragon's fiery breath on my fingers.

Across the moonlit battlements we ran, down a spiral staircase, across a banqueting hall, and through a secret passage on the other side of a tapestry. And the whole time I could hear and feel and even *smell* the evil dragon following in close pursuit.

'The dungeons,' Sir Sebastian cried out. 'They're our only hope.'

We went down the cold stone steps, swords drawn. The cries of imprisoned men, women and children filled the chilly damp air. Suddenly, the dragon appeared at the end of the corridor. Massive it was, with teeth the size of daggers and claws like carving-knives. It was fast, too, despite its size. Before we even had time to turn around, the dragon was on us.

I swung my sword. I parried and thrust. But it was no good. The dragon was only interested in Sebastian, and there was nothing I could do to prevent it getting him.

GAME OVER.

This time, the message in the printer was a little longer. BETTER LUCK NEXT TIME. LET'S HOPE IT'S THIRD TIME LUCKY, EH? PLEASE DON'T GIVE UP ON ME, MICHAEL. OTHERWISE I'LL HAVE TO STAY LOCKED UP IN HERE FOR EVER. TRY 'JAILBREAK'. I THINK IT MIGHT JUST WORK! CHEERS, SEB.

I didn't even bother to read the rules of *Jailbreak* before going in. I knew that whatever the computer said, *my* task would be to rescue the boy. And sure enough, my cellmate was prisoner 02478: Schultz.

'I've got to get out of here,' Sebastian sighed. 'Are you going to help?'

'Of course I am,' I said. 'Have you got a plan?'

Stupid question. With the help of a skeleton swipecard, we were soon out of the cell and racing down corridors. Sirens wailed, guard dogs howled, heavy boots came tramping. Behind us, steel-barred doors slammed shut, one after the other. We dodged the guards, we fled the dogs, we made it to a staircase and pounded upwards.

On the roof, Sebastian looked round at the horizon and glanced at his watch nervously. 'It should be here by now.'

'What?' I said.

'That!' said Sebastian and pointed. I saw a small dot in the sky, and heard a distant *chugga-chugga*, which was getting louder by the second.

'A helicopter!' I exclaimed.

'That was *my* idea!' said Sebastian excitedly. 'If only it would go a bit faster . . .'

At that moment, the door behind us burst open. Twelve guards with twelve vicious dogs were standing there. As I watched in horror, the guards bent down and unclicked the dogs' leads. The next instant they were hurtling across the roof towards us, all bared teeth and dripping jowls. Out of the corner of my eye, I saw Sebastian take a step backwards.

'NOOOOOO!' I screamed.

But it was too late. The boy had slipped from the roof and was already tumbling back through the air, down to the concrete below.

GAME OVER.

As I removed the visor, I looked in the printer tray. This time it was empty. I felt really bad. I'd failed Sebastian; I'd failed the game. It was only later, when the scenes began to fade in my memory, that it occurred to me that Sebastian Schultz *was* the game.

Strangely, though, although I went back to *Wildwest*, *Dragonquest* and *Jailbreak* after that, I never met up with Sebastian again. Dad said it must have been a glitch, but I wasn't convinced.

Then, yesterday, I heard from Sebastian again. It was Wednesday, and I'd got home early from games. I went straight up to the Powerbase and there, in the printer tray, was a sheet of paper.

CAN WE HAVE ONE LAST TRY? it said. I THINK THE HELICOPTER WAS THE RIGHT IDEA, BUT ESCAPING FROM A PRISON WAS WRONG. THERE'S GOT TO BE SOME KIND OF AN ACCIDENT . . . GO INTO 'WARZONE'. IF THIS DOESN'T WORK I WON'T BOTHER YOU AGAIN. CHEERS, SEB.

I couldn't tell which war zone we were in. Basically, it was a city somewhere. The tall buildings were windowless and riddled with holes. Machine-gun fire raked the sky. Walls tumbled. Bombs exploded. All I knew was that Sebastian and I had to make it to that helicopter in one piece.

Heads down and arms raised, we ran across a no-man's-land of rubble and smoke, dodging sniper fire as we did so. At the far end we went through a door in a wall. The helicopter was on the ground about three hundred metres away, propeller a blur, waiting for our arrival.

We started to run, but the tank fire sent us scuttling back to the wall.

'A Jeep,' Sebastian shouted to me, and nodded at a camouflage-green vehicle parked by the road. 'Just what we need!'

'I can't drive,' I said.

'Neither can I,' said Sebastian. 'But we've got no other choice.' He jumped in, turned the ignition key and revved the engine. 'Jump in!'

I climbed into the passenger seat, and we were off.

'Uh oh,' said Sebastian, glancing in his mirror. 'There's a tank behind us.'

I spun round. The tank was hurtling along after us at a terrific speed. Not only did we have to go like maniacs,

but Sebastian had to keep swerving this way and that to avoid the shells being fired at us.

Suddenly, with the helicopter only ten metres away, Sebastian slammed on the brakes and sent the Jeep skidding into a spin. I leapt clear, scrambled up and jumped into the waiting helicopter.

'Made it!' I said. The helicopter immediately started to go upwards. I looked around. Sebastian wasn't there. 'Wait!' I shouted at the pilot.

I looked back. The Jeep had stopped, but Sebastian hadn't got out. The tank was bearing down on him.

'COME ON!' I yelled. But Sebastian didn't move. Sitting staring at the oncoming tank, it was as if his body had been turned to stone.

All at once, the air was filled with the sickening crunch of metal on metal as the tank crashed into the side of the Jeep. I saw Sebastian's face fill with panic and confusion as he was thrown up out of his seat and into the air.

Round and round he tumbled, over and over – closer and closer to the helicopter. He landed with a thud on the ground, just below the hatch. I leant down quickly, grabbed him by the wrist and pulled him up. Not a moment too soon. As he sat down beside me, the helicopter soared up into the sky.

I'd done it. I'd rescued Sebastian at last. Before I had a chance to say anything to him though, the helicopter flew into thick cloud. It poured in through the open door and turned everything blinding white. I couldn't see a thing – until 'GAME OVER' flashed up.

When I removed the visor, the screen was flashing a score of 40,000,000.

Forty million! I'd hit the jackpot. I'd finally cracked the game.

*

At least, that was what I thought then. Now I knew that Sebastian Schultz, the boy from the game, really did exist. I'd seen the proof in the newspaper.

But how? I wondered as I got off the train. What was going on?

Questions I had plenty of. It was time for some answers. Home at last, I raced up to the Powerbase and checked the printer. There was nothing there waiting for me. Feeling a bit miffed, I went into the Net instead. I wanted to learn more about the MIRACLE RECOVERY story.

I found what I was looking for quickly enough – and there was far more there than in the woman's newspaper. It was on page two that something interesting caught my eye. As I read on, my head started reeling.

Apparently, at the time of the accident, Sebastian was using his laptop to play one of the same psycho-drive games that I've got.

My heart pounded furiously. I felt hot and cold all over. What if . . . ? No, it was too incredible . . . But the thought would not go away.

What if, because Sebastian had been plugged into the computer when he'd banged his head in the accident, the computer had saved *his* memory in its own? And if that was the case, then what if the weird versions of the games *I'd* been drawn into – *Wildwest* and *Dragonquest*, *Jailbreak* and *Warzone* – had all been attempts to retrieve that memory?

After all, what's it Dad's always saying about the computer's memory? 'It can never forget, Michael. Nothing ever gets lost.'

The thing is, I thought, even if it was somehow possible that Sebastian's memory had been stored on disk, then how had it ended up on *my* computer? Scrolling down the article, I discovered a possible explanation on the final page.

Answering a reporter's question as to what the family was going to do next, Mr Schultz said that they were off to DCL Computers to stock up on some games. 'It was while we were in the hospital. Someone broke into the car and stole the lot. I don't know what happened to them.'

'I do,' I said quietly. 'They ended up at the Computer Fair. And *we* bought them.'

Having finished the article, I left the Net and checked my e-mail. There were two letters. One from my uncle David in New York. And one from Sebastian.

Of course, I thought. It was stupid of me to expect a letter in the printer tray. How could there have been? Sebastian had escaped. With trembling fingers I clicked in, and read the message.

DEAR MICHAEL, it said. THANK YOU! I'M NOT REALLY SURE HOW IT HAPPENED – EITHER(?), BUT THANKS. YOU SAVED MY LIFE. LET'S MEET UP SOME TIME SOON. WE NEED TO TALK – BUT DON'T MENTION ANY OF THIS TO ANYONE ELSE. IT'LL ONLY FREAK THEM OUT. CHEERS, SEB. P.S. KEEP THE GAMES. YOU'VE EARNED THEM.

I shook my head in amazement. A real message from the real Sebastian Schultz. Even though he didn't understand it any more than I did, we both knew that by reliving the accident, *something* had happened. Something weird, something wonderful – something that should have been impossible. But then again, as Dad says, 'Now that there are two advanced intelligences on earth, who can say what is and what isn't possible?'

All I know is this. Everything that I've described is true. Virtually.

Activities

Brian and the Brain by Janet Burchett and Sara Vogler

1 **In a pair**, describe how to play one of your own computer games OR one of your favourite arcade games. Assume that your partner knows nothing about it.

Say what the object of the game is, how it works, and how you score points (or win). Answer your partner's questions and explain why you enjoy playing it.

2 Pretend that you and your partner manufacture and sell the computer games Brian collects. Choose ONE from those mentioned in the story: *Space Bowls*, *Marauding Martians*, *Attack of the Killer Klingfilms*, *Thundering Terrapins* and *Nova-nerds from Neptune*.

a Produce an instruction leaflet to accompany the game you choose. You first need to discuss exactly what points it should cover. Aim for a good balance between words and illustrations. If you wish, create it on screen.

b Plan an advertising campaign to promote the game to young people aged 11–14. Decide whether you want to produce a TV commercial or a full-page advert for a magazine.

You could script a 30-second TV ad; invent a catchy slogan and/or jingle; design a magazine illustration with an advertising text of about 50 words . . . and so on. The more you use your own ideas, the better your advert will be.

3 On page 10, when Brian still has 'the Brain', his mother is searching the family computer for her children's story *Ellie and the Elves*:

'Up came the title – *Ellie and the Elves Get Beaten Up*. There followed grisly descriptions of packs of avenging pixies and disembowelled elves hanging from trees.'

In a small group, talk about some stories you remember reading, or having read to you, when you were much younger. Then share ideas about what they would have been like if they'd been written as **horror** stories. (You could ask your teacher to read aloud any of Roald Dahl's *Revolting Rhymes* to get you in the mood.)

Then **on your own**, write your version of EITHER *Ellie and the Elves Get Beaten Up* OR a fairy-tale you remember from childhood retold as a horror story.

4 Imagine that, like Brian, you are working on a computer when you find yourself able to perform several of its functions. Some of these should differ from the ones Brian is capable of in the story. Some can be the same.

In a pair, take turns to describe a day in your life. It need not be a school day. Then **on your own** write about some of the things that happen to you EITHER in story form OR as several scenes from a play.

5 Brian the Brain receives a number of e-mails. Look back through the story to remind yourself of who sends them and what they say.

On your own, pretend you are Brian the Brain. Write replies to two of the e-mails. Do this in a deliberately mischievous way that will cause major confusion and/or embarrassment.

Faces by Dennis Hamley

1 **In a small group**, talk about the 'egg-faces' in this story. Give your ideas about:

- who they might be

- where they might come from

- what non-human powers they have

- why they recapture the man at the end of the story

- what plans they may have for the future.

Would you describe *Faces* as a science-fiction story? Give reasons for your opinion by comparing it with other sci-fi stories you know.

2 **In a pair**, pretend you are CID officers in the area where this story is set. During the last month about twenty people have been reported missing. Several have reappeared. They claim to have been kidnapped, like the man in the story, by strangers with faces 'smooth and featureless as an egg'.

You decide to produce a WARNING poster to be displayed in the area telling people of the danger they may be in. It should give accurate information but be designed not to alarm the public (especially children) too much. Create the poster, using up to 50 words. Do it on a computer if you wish.

3 **In a pair**, act out an interview between a journalist on the local newspaper and someone who was captured by egg-faces but escaped.

Then **on your own** write a front-page story based on this interview. Use the headline:

POLICE FAIL TO CRACK EGG-FACE MYSTERY

– PANIC SPREADS

4 **In a small group**, imagine you are going to read this
     story aloud to a class of your own age.

     To add to the suspense you decide to read it in *six*
     sections. After each section (except the last) you will stop
     and ask them:

     • what they think is happening, and why

     • what they predict is going to happen next.

     Discuss and agree on the five points where you will halt
     the reading. Then decide what questions you are going
     to ask about each section. For instance, after reading the
     first one you could ask:

     • *Why do you think the man running along the road is
       so agitated?*

     • *What do you notice about how the car driver is
       dressed?*

     • *Is there anything surprising about the way the driver
       speaks?*

     • *What might happen once the man has got into the
       car?*

     After writing down your questions, arrange to present
     the story in this way to a group from another class. At
     the end, ask them how much they enjoyed it – and why.

Banana by Neil Arksey

1   **In a pair**, re-read the descriptions of the 'friendly' football game (pages 19–20) and the penalty shoot-out (pages 28–30).

Pretend you are football commentators. Decide which of the above episodes each of you will cover. Get familiar with it by making brief notes on the action it describes. Then do a live commentary on it lasting 2–3 minutes, preferably onto audio-tape.

On your own, select in advance a televised football match or another sporting event which interests you. At home, watch part of it with the sound turned down. Tape-record your own commentary for between 5 and 10 minutes. You could give the tape to your teacher to assess your Speaking and Listening skills.

2   **In a pair**, act out the conversation between Mr Drisco and one of Titch Wilson's parents at the next school Parents' Evening.

Remember that Mr Drisco teaches Titch physics *and* runs the First Eleven. What will he have to say about Titch? What will Titch's father or mother want to ask?

On your own, write an end-of-year report for Titch as if you are Mr Drisco.

3   The illustration on the front cover of this book is based on the ending of *Banana*. **On your own**, EITHER draw your own version of it OR illustrate another part of the story. Then imagine you are editing a collection of sporting stories which includes *Banana*. Write a 50-word 'blurb' about the story for the book's back cover. Try to arouse your readers' interest in it without giving away the ending.

4   **In a small group**, talk about some sporting stories you have read which would make an interesting collection for readers aged 11–14. Why do *you* enjoy them? Why might other people like them too?

Bring copies of your favourite stories into class. Read them around the group. Then choose between five and eight of them for a new collection to be called EITHER *Best Sports Stories Ever* OR a title you invent yourselves.

Arrange to try out your collection on another class. Think of a way of recording new readers' reactions. You could make up a questionnaire for them to fill in, then record their answers in the form of tables, bar graphs, pie charts, etc.

Imagine that your collection is going to be published. (Better still, ask your teacher to have a 'limited edition' printed in school.) There are a number of tasks to share between you – e.g. designing the front cover, illustrating each story, creating the Contents page, writing an Introduction, producing an advert to go in the publisher's catalogue (or to display in school).

5 The title of *Banana* does not tell you straight away what the story is about. What did *you* think when you first saw it?

In a small group, look at the other titles below. Talk about how suitable they would be for the story. Decide on a mark out of 5 for each (1 = 'hopeless'; 5 = 'excellent').

- A Lesson for Mr Drisco
- The Goalie Who Grew Up
- Watch it, Batesy!
- The Science of Soccer
- The Goalkeeper's Revenge
- Size Doesn't Matter!

The Bakerloo Flea by Michael Rosen

In a small group, pretend you are the production team employed to make a video film of *The Bakerloo Flea*. Do some or all of the following tasks:

a **As a group**, create a storyboard for your video film. If this is a new activity to you, your teacher will explain how to go about it.

Draw a sequence of between six and ten frames. Divide up the work between you. The caption for each frame should be limited to *one* sentence.

b **With a partner**, draw up a cast list of human characters. Then discuss which actors you will invite to play these parts. If you don't know their real names, refer to them by the names of characters they play in TV programmes or films you have seen.

Re-form your group. Take it in turns to explain your choice of actors. Reach a final decision about casting (take a vote if necessary), then make out a cast list to be printed in the film's publicity material. Go on to talk about a suitable costume for each character.

c **With a partner**, plan and write part of the film script.

Read aloud the ending of the story from 'Vera's old man . . .' (page 37) to ' "You've got him, love, you've got him!" ' (page 38). Your script should be based on this passage. First, discuss which characters will speak, then what they will say. Apart from two lines, you need to invent all the *dialogue* (i.e. conversation). Write or type it out. Then, with the help of others in your group, act it onto audio- or videotape.

d **On your own**, make a design sketch of the Flea. Check the story for details of what it looks like and how it moves. If you like, look up a picture of a flea in your school or local library. You may want to label different parts of your sketch. Beneath it, write precise instructions to help the designer make a realistic working model for use during filming.

e **As a group**, divide up between you the following jobs, all of which are necessary to publicize and 'package' your film:

- creating advertising posters and 'small ads'

- writing letters to the managers of video shops giving advice about how to promote the film

- designing the video box in which it will be sold

- producing a summary sheet (100–150 words) of the film's plot, to be read by critics who will review it.

Star Pupil by Lorna Read

1 Early in the story Spike finds problems in behaving like a normal Earth pupil.

In a pair, remind yourself of the things Spike gets wrong. Talk about the reasons for his mistakes. What other things not mentioned in the story would you guess he found difficulty with?

Pretend that a disguised alien joins *your* class. Make up *An Alien's Guide to Our School* to help him or her fit in without the teachers noticing. Produce it on a computer if you wish.

Exactly what you put in your *Alien's Guide* is up to you. It might be helpful to include:

- an explanation of any strange 'Earth-words' or phrases the alien might hear during a typical day in your class

- advice on how to get on with (or avoid upsetting) certain pupils and teachers

- an unofficial map showing parts of the school which it would be best not to visit, with explanations.

2 During an art lesson, Spike uses his mental powers to bring up on his friends' computer screens pictures of what they most want to be (see pages 42–44). Later on he tells them: 'I just read your fantasies.'

On your own, imagine you have the same powers as Spike. Create on screen or on paper an image of one of *your* friend's daydreams about the future. Underneath the image, write a description of:

(i) what it shows

(ii) why you have chosen it.

If you wish, you could also do one about yourself.

3 Spike's friends believe he returned to Karn 'because of the media attention':

> '. . . the local press and TV, then the nationals, got wind of the story.'

In a pair, pretend you are news reporters for your local TV station. Following the events on Sports Day, you are sent to the school to investigate rumours of 'alien powers'.

Prepare a 3-minute news item to be filmed live from the school. Write the script between you. You may want to include interviews: if so, arrange for others in your class to help.

Rehearse your report carefully, then act it out in front of an audience. It would be ideal if you could actually have it filmed.

4 **In a small group**, re-read the *Report on Spikemarnio L. Kalendreth* (pages 50–51) and the fax Lee gets from Spike at the end of the story.

Pretend you are some of the Earth pupils in Spike's class. Between you, write a letter of reply to be sent to him in Karn via the Omni-Translator. In the letter you could:

- bring Spike up to date with the latest news from school

- remind him of some of the best things that happened when he was in your class

- look forward to sharing more adventures when you see him again next term.

Needle by Alan Gibbons

1 **In a small group**, talk about the ups and downs of Terry's life in the course of this story. When is he at his most 'up', and why? When is he at his most 'down', and why?

Look at **Episodes A to F** in turn. They are:

Episode A – *Terry hears he is moving to Liverpool*

Episode B – *Terry first meets Chris Doherty at school*

Episode C – *Terry starts training with Tommy Mac*

Episode D – *Terry spars with 'the big feller'*

Episode E – *Terry scraps with Chris Doherty at school*

Episode F – *Terry prepares for his bout against Connolly*

Each make an enlarged copy of the bar graph below:

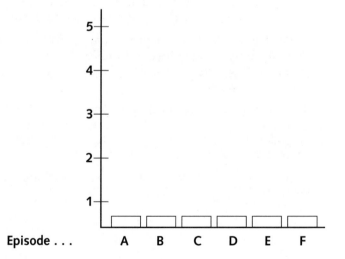

Show what you think about Terry's 'ups' and 'downs' by drawing bars on your graph for each Episode. Talk together about how high to draw them. A bar that reaches 5 means 'very far up'; one that only reaches 1 means 'very far down'.

2 **In a pair**, discuss what the story shows about Tommy Mac's way of training youngsters to box. Find examples from the text. What opinion do you have about Tommy's methods? Do you think they would work for *you*?

Pretend that you are Tommy Mac. **On your own**, produce an A4 leaflet entitled *Five Ways to be a Winner*. The leaflet will be given out to all future members of the Boxing Club.

Base your leaflet on the facts in the story. It will benefit from being illustrated. Design and produce it to look as professional as possible.

3 **In class discussion**, put forward your ideas about the moral (or message) of this story. As people make suggestions, your teacher could write them on the board, on an overhead projector, on large pieces of card, etc.

Make sure you back up everything you say with evidence from the story. Round off your discussion by saying how true to life you consider the story's message – or messages – to be.

4 **In a small group**, act out a situation in which someone proves to be a 'winner' in an unexpected way or against the odds. The situation is up to you to create: it need not involve physical conflict.

Your group can work to a script OR do an improvisation.

Mayday! by Redvers Brandling

1 **In a pair**, use an atlas to trace Captain Sercombe's flight from take-off in Singapore to the landing at Jakarta airport.

   Working together, draw a flight map which includes labels to show:

   - the changing weather conditions during the flight

   - where the plane's engine problems occurred

   - where, and by how much, the plane lost height

   - anything else you consider important.

   When you have finished, join up with another pair and compare maps. If there are differences, find out why.

2 **On your own**, imagine you are Captain Sercombe. After the unscheduled landing at Jakarta, you are told to write a flight report for your airline's Official Investigators. They need a full account of what happened to the Boeing 747 between take-off and landing.

   First go through the story and make notes on the facts you will put into your report. Decide for yourself how much detail to include. It is vital to the investigation that these facts are *accurate*.

   Now make a decision about whether your report will be fully *truthful*. (Remember that, as far as the crew is concerned, you were alone on the flight deck when the engines re-fired.) As an airline pilot, how much is it in your interests to tell?

   When you have completed your notes, write up the report in a clear and straightforward style.

Worms by John Gatehouse

1   **In a pair**, find the points in the story where the following extracts occur:

  (i) 'I'm sending a note home to your parents,' Mr Hunter told him. 'And you will not be going to the ice rink with the rest of your class on Friday.'

  (ii) 'I'm suspending you for a week,' said Mr Hunter . . . 'And I'll be phoning your mother to let her know why you're not in school.'

  Discuss what Mr Hunter will say in his note and phone call. You first need to check what's happening in the story at points (i) and (ii). How do you think Jeremy's parents will react?

  Improvise the phone call from Mr Hunter telling Jeremy's mother that he is suspended. What will they both say – and what tone of voice will they use to say it?

  Then act out the conversation between Jeremy and his father on the same evening. How will each of them feel about Jeremy's suspension?

2   **On your own**, make up a short story in which a group of animals or insects take revenge on someone who has been cruel to them.

  Make it a gory story. You could call it 'The *spiders* OR *frogs* OR *wasps* OR *caterpillars* OR *maggots* OR *??* fight back' . . . or invent a title of your own.

  If you wish, write it as a nightmare like the ones Jeremy has in the story.

Cocky and Clive by Robert Swindells

1 **In a pair**, pretend you are making a short documentary film for Schools Television about being a fighter pilot in the Second World War. Your film will be based on what Cocky says about his experience of flying Hurricanes on pages 81–82 of the story. Re-read it now.

You are going to include in your film:

- some clips showing fighter pilots in action

- an interview with a pilot from Cocky's squadron who is still alive.

Decide on a title for your film. Then make out a storyboard for the film clips you are going to use. Write the voice-over commentary to accompany them.

Act out and tape your interview with the fighter pilot. One of you plays his part, the other puts questions to him. Working together, script this interview and rehearse it several times before recording it.

2 At the start of the story Jim and Clive are enemies. By the end they have become best friends. Fifty years later, they still are.

In class discussion, talk about why this happened. How did their experiences during the war bring them closer together? What did the war make them realize about themselves and about each other?

At the end of the story Jim says, 'Makes you wonder why we had to fight in the first place, doesn't it?' Exchange ideas about what *you* think about war and fighting after reading this story.

Chicken by Mary Hoffman

1 **In a small group**, pretend you are members of the Inliners gang. You keep a *Dare Diary* of all the dares people in your gang carry out. It has four columns:

- Particular dare carried out.

- Reasons for doing it.

- How successful was it?

- Any other comments.

Look back through the story. Remind yourself of the Inliners' dares it describes. Then, between you, use the headings above to fill in your *Dare Diary*.

2 The newspapers report what happened at Silbury cuttings:

'The local papers tried to turn Alfie into a hero' (page 95).

In a pair, imagine you are both journalists on one of the local papers. Write a front-page story about the accident, using the headline:

SCHOOLBOYS IN RAILWAY LINE DRAMA

Check the story to make sure your facts are correct. You could include interviews with Alfie, Dylan, the train driver and Mrs Nixon. Will the two boys tell the *full* story about why the accident happened?

If you wish, use a computer to produce your front-page story. It should be illustrated.

Barney by Will Stanton

1 **In a small group**, talk about the last diary entry, for 11 September. Share your ideas about:

- how it differs from the other diary entries

- who has written it, and how this is possible

- why it includes a request to 'bring the young ratts like I said. Just females'.

2 **In a pair**, imagine that Barney is able to read and write from the beginning of the story. Like the scientist, he also keeps a diary. Between you, write the five entries he makes in it from 30 August to 10 September inclusive.

Describe any aspects of life on the island you wish, as well as Barney's private thoughts and feelings. He will probably give his own reactions to the events mentioned by the scientist in *his* diary.

3 **On your own**, imagine that enough time has passed since 11 September for all of Barney's requests to be granted. The island rats are now ready to mount a full-scale attack against humans.

Write an account of what happens, using the title *The Rat Revolution*.

4 Among other things, *Barney* is a story about the use of animals for scientific experiments. **In a small group**, create a pamphlet to persuade people that this is wrong. You will need to do some research for this: ask your teacher for advice and share the task between you. Include in your pamphlet illustrations, statistics, quotations, etc., and write in a style designed to shock your readers. Use a computer to produce your final version.

Virtually True by Paul Stewart

1 In his final message to Michael (page 115), Sebastian says:

> 'I'M NOT REALLY SURE HOW IT HAPPENED –
> EITHER (?), BUT THANKS. YOU SAVED MY
> LIFE. LET'S MEET UP SOME TIME SOON. WE NEED
> TO TALK.'

In a pair, act out the meeting Sebastian suggests. One of you plays Michael, and the other Sebastian.

During your meeting, talk about:

- Sebastian's experiences 'inside' the computer games

- how he came to be there

- how Michael gradually realized something strange was going on

- the importance of Michael's visit to Rigby Computer Fair

- Michael's dad's comments about 'two advanced intelligences on earth' (page 115).

2 **On your own**, imagine you have an experience like Sebastian's. In some way (work this out for yourself) you get 'stuck' inside EITHER one of your own computer games OR one of those owned by Michael – *Tornado*, *Megabash*, *Scum City*, *Black Belt* or *Kyrene's Kastle*.

Describe what happens to you. In the end, do you get rescued as Sebastian did – or do you remain trapped in the game for ever? Whatever you decide, make sure your story has a dramatic and unusual ending.

3 **In a pair**, look back to the newspaper report about Sebastian's MIRACLE RECOVERY on page 103 of the story.

Only the first part of it is printed. Talk about what the rest of the report might say. Your knowledge of the whole story will help you to work this out.

On your own, copy out the newspaper report as far as it goes. Then carry it on to the end, writing in the same style. Among other things, you could include in it interviews with:

- Sebastian's parents, Mr and Mrs Schultz

- a doctor at the hospital where Sebastian was in a coma

- Sebastian himself after his recovery.

Produce your completed report in newspaper format, ideally on a computer. It is important enough to be a front-page story: you will need a main headline, sub-heads, pictures with captions, paragraph headings, etc.

4 As its title suggests, this story is about virtual reality.

In class discussion, share your knowledge of the ways in which computer experts use virtual-reality techniques. To what uses are they already being put? To what further uses do you think they might be put in the future?

Then hold a debate on the subject:

This class believes that the development of virtual reality on computers is likely to do more harm than good.

Smash!

By Robert Swindells

The fuse was burning now, yellow flame climbing hungrily towards the bottle neck. He drew back his arm and threw without aiming. The bottle arced through the air trailing sparks . . .

When two young children are the victims of a racial attack, it leads friends Steve and Ashraf to question their friendship and loyalties. As their anger at events develops they find themselves getting drawn into a world of hatred and violence that threatens to destroy not only their friendship but the lives of those around them . . .

Age 12+   ISBN: 0 435 12501 X

*Josh groped his way out of sleep,
immediately remembering that the twins
had a secret.*

Josh knows his brothers are hiding
something from him – something so big
and terrible that it is making Tom
remote and Jack violent.

Struggling to understand what it is that is
changing them . . . making them
wicked . . . Josh is determined to get to
the bottom of their secret. But is he
prepared for the terrible truth of what
they have done?

Age 13+   ISBN: 0 435 12505 2

Founding Editors: Anne and Ian Serraillier

Chinua Achebe Things Fall Apart
David Almond Skellig
Maya Angelou I Know Why the Caged Bird Sings
Margaret Atwood The Handmaid's Tale
Jane Austen Pride and Prejudice
Stan Barstow Joby: A Kind of Loving
Nina Bawden Carrie's War; The Finding; Humbug
Malorie Blackman Tell Me No Lies; Words Last Forever
Charlotte Brontë Jane Eyre
Emily Brontë Wuthering Heights
Melvin Burgess and Lee Hall Billy Elliot
Betsy Byars The Midnight Fox; The Pinballs; The Eighteenth Emergency
Victor Canning The Runaways
Sir Arthur Conan Doyle Sherlock Holmes Short Stories
Susan Cooper King of Shadows
Robert Cormier Heroes
Roald Dahl Danny; The Champion of the World; The Wonderful
Story of Henry Sugar; George's Marvellous Medicine; The Witches;
Boy; Going Solo; Matilda; My Year
Anita Desai The Village by the Sea
Charles Dickens A Christmas Carol; Great Expectations; A Charles
Dickens Selection
Berlie Doherty Granny was a Buffer Girl; Street Child
Roddy Doyle Paddy Clarke Ha Ha Ha
George Eliot Silas Marner
Anne Fine The Granny Project
Leon Garfield Six Shakespeare Stories
Ann Halam Dr Franklin's Island
Thomas Hardy The Withered Arm and Other Wessex Tales; The Mayor
of Casterbridge
Ernest Hemmingway The Old Man and the Sea; A Farewell to Arms
Barry Hines A Kestrel For A Knave
Nigel Hinton Buddy; Buddy's Song
Anne Holm I Am David

Janni Howker Badger on the Barge; The Nature of the Beast; Martin Farrell
Pete Johnson The Protectors
Geraldine Kaye Comfort Herself
Daniel Keyes Flowers for Algernon
Dick King-Smith The Sheep-Pig
Elizabeth Laird Red Sky in the Morning
D H Lawrence The Fox and The Virgin and the Gypsy; Selected Tales
Harper Lee To Kill a Mockingbird
C Day Lewis The Otterbury Incident
Joan Linguard Across the Barricades
Penelope Lively The Ghost of Thomas Kemp
Geraldine McCaughrean Stories from Shakespeare; Pack of Lies
Bernard MacLaverty Cal; The Best of Bernard MacLaverty
Jan Mark Heathrow Nights
James Vance Marshall Walkabout
Ian McEwan The Daydreamer; A Child in Time
Michael Morpurgo The Wreck of the Zanzibar; Why the Whales Came; Arthur, High King of Britain; Kensuke's Kingdom; From Hereabout Hill; Robin of Sherwood
Beverley Naidoo No Turning Back; The Other Side of Truth
Bill Naughton The Goalkeeper's Revenge
New Windmill A Charles Dickens Selection
New Windmill Anthology of Challenging Texts: Thoughtlines
New Windmill Book of Classic Short Stories
New Windmill Book of Fiction and Non-fiction: Taking Off!
New Windmill Book of Greek Myths
New Windmill Book of Haunting Tales
New Windmill Book of Humorous Stories: Don't Make Me Laugh
New Windmill Book of Nineteenth Century Short Stories
New Windmill Book of Non-fiction: Get Real
New Windmill Book of Non-fiction: Real Lives, Real Times
New Windmill Book of Scottish Short Stories
New Windmill Book of Short Stories: Fast and Curious
New Windmill Book of Short Stories: From Beginning to End
New Windmill Book of Short Stories: Into the Unknown
New Windmill Book of Short Stories: Tales with a Twist
New Windmill Book of Short Stories: Trouble in Two Centuries
New Windmill Book of Short Stories: Ways with Words
New Windmill Book of Stories from Many Cultures and Traditions; Fifty-Fifty Tuti-Fruity Chocolate Chip

How many have you read?